NADINE LITTLE

We Are Not Broken

The Warrior Angels 2

LITTLE PUBLISHING

Sign up to my mailing list to get a free bonus epilogue. Members of my mailing list get other free stuff and exclusive behind-the-scenes material.

Members are always the first to hear about my new books and discounts.

See the back of the book for details on how to join.

'Some things, once taken, can never be returned.
Some things, once broken, are broken forever.'
Maiya Ibrahim, *Spice Road*.

'You could burn me a thousand times
and I would still want you as my own.'
Claire Legrand, *Lightbringer*

1

"Do you, Maia Buckthorn, take Hunter... um... the semi-indestructible warrior angel, to be your lawfully wedded husband?"

The priest's words drift to the lofty rafters and echo over the heads of everybody gathered in the pews. A fist muffles a cough. Feathers rustle. Ruby- and emerald-dappled sunlight brightens the rear of the church and casts a shadow around the statue above the altar. Black wings spread wide, the face chiselled in marble. The figure grips a blue sword, the blade pointed downwards to a swirl of Latin script at his booted feet: *Ordo sanctorum angelorum.*

The Order of the Holy Angels. Or, as I like to call it—my dad's zealous worship of the angels and their grudging tolerance of it.

I squeeze the warm hand in mine and say, "I do."

Steph, my best friend in this universe and all the rest, sniffles on my left. She dabs her eyes with a tissue, my bouquet of snowdrops and crocuses clenched in her other hand on top of her diamond-bedazzled cane. Her sapphire wig tumbles down her back almost to the low cut of her midnight-blue dress.

She lasted longer than I thought she would. Wedding rehearsals are unusual in Scotland but we held a run-through a week ago for the benefit of Hunter and the other angels, whose culture has no such thing as marriage or love, only dominance and brutality. Steph started bawling as soon as I walked down the aisle on the arm of my dad, even though I was wearing jeans and a hoodie, my hair pinned messily thanks to Hunter's wandering hands and enthusiasm at desecrating the confessional situated off the antechamber.

He likes to get grabby in cramped, dark places. And, since he's the holiest of Holy Angels, it's technically his church so he can do whatever the hell he wants in it. Including me.

Greg, fellow Martello Court resident and rebel, rolls his shoulders next to Steph in his charcoal suit and tie, the shirt matching the colour of Steph's dress. He's been grumbling about how uncomfortable it is all morning. His long hair is held back, one hand clasped over the other, as if his tattoo of a spiderweb might offend the eyeballs of the priest.

The minister is holding his own, though, in what has become a very unorthodox ceremony. It's been an unorthodox couple of years, what with the angel apocalypse and all.

The priest raises his gaze from me. He blinks fast, his throat bobbing. Vestments whisper on the floor as he shifts.

"And do you, Hunter, take Maia Buckthorn"—a slight hesitation and clearing of the throat—"the fragile human, to be your lawfully wedded wife?"

I fold my lips to hide a smirk at the priest's stuttering over the inside joke in our vows.

He followed my dad in forming the Order as an off-shoot of the Catholic church, with the angels as our modern-day saints. Not everyone is happy with their focus of worship. To them, Dad says God created all things, even the Creators and especially the angels they made.

I slide my gaze to my almost-husband on my right. Black hair falls into dark, unflinching eyes. Hunter's midnight-blue shirt hugs his shoulders, his wings tucked to his back and shimmering purple and green in the light. He's wearing the same laced boots and trousers since we first met, when he tried to dust me with an arrow. I can get him out of them for sex but not for his own wedding, or much else. Except maybe a foot rub, though that inevitably leads to the sex thing.

Just one of his adorable quirks.

"I take," Hunter says in his soft, low voice. The slight growl pulses heat to places it shouldn't when I'm standing in a church in front of friends, allies, angels and my own father.

I shiver in my dress, the white silk softened by the delicate embroidered leaves and flowers in jade and gold. Hunter's fingers tighten in mine. His thumb brushes my palm, and my thighs tense.

Steph huffs a watery sigh into her tissue and makes googly eyes at Devinon, the warrior angel next to Hunter. Since Hunter is so tall and broad, all I get are flashes of sapphire wings and blond, shoulder-length hair. I assume my dad is still on Dev's right, looking sprightly in his beige tunic patterned with thread honouring our colour scheme.

He was ecstatic to stand on the groom's side even if it was only for the symmetry. His worship of Hunter hasn't waned in the fourteen months he's known him.

The priest's eyes flick between me and Hunter.

"Then, may the Lord strengthen the consent you have declared before our church and bring to fulfilment his blessings with you." He guides his attention to the small group in the pews. "What our Order has joined, let no one put asunder."

Another shiver prickles down my spine, less pleasant than

the promise of being claimed by Hunter.

The priest claps, and I flinch. Hunter cocks his head.

"Now let us proceed to the blessing and giving of rings." The priest beckons with his fingers.

Devinon skips forward to hand him a cloth bag, a proud grin on his face at remembering his role. His outfit is the same as Greg's, though the shirt and suit jacket had to be cut up the back and re-pinned around his wings.

Two circlets of black zirconium spill into the priest's waiting palm. "May the Lord bless these rings so that those who wear them abide in love and peace."

Planning the wedding tested my newly rekindled relationship with my dad. I let him persuade me to use his church now that it worships the angels but I refused to budge on cutting out most of the God and babies stuff of regular Catholicism, especially since Hunter is infertile. A weapon created for war has no need to produce offspring. Dad babbled about adoption and surrogacy until I told him to zip it. There would also be no singing or prayers or readings, just a simple ceremony in front of a select group—the twenty jewel-winged warrior angels who remained behind after their creators tried to call them back, and ten of Martello Court's finest.

I think we've pulled it off beautifully.

Holy water sprinkles the bands. Hunter plucks my smaller ring from the priest's hand and I swipe his, running a shaking finger over the topaz gems and delicate motif of a planet, a star and a feather. I hold my left hand out to Hunter.

"Maia," he says, staring at me with his usual brain-dissecting intensity, "this ring is a symbol of my love and protection. I am yours, forever and always."

The circlet slides onto my finger. My heart skips.

"Hunter," I squeak. I clear my throat and repeat his name at a more acceptable decibel. His hand is steady in mine as I slip the band on. "This ring is a symbol of my love and protection. I am yours, forever and always."

Steph blubbers into her tissue. Greg attempts to turn a sniff into a cough, and chokes on his own bodily fluids. Hunter tugs me flush against his solid heat.

The priest stutters. "You may kiss—"

"I like kissing," Hunter says.

He dips his head and seals his mouth over mine. His wings flare at my moan. My eyes shut, and the sounds of celebration fade. Nothing exists but Hunter's soft lips and the wicked glide of his tongue. My arms wind around his neck. His hands find my waist and lift me higher, my feet off the floor, my hips pressed to his erection. I grind against him.

"Uh, Maia," Steph chuckles, "if you could stop humping your indestructible angel husband for one second…"

I gasp and wrench my mouth from Hunter's. He relaxes his grip to let me slide all the way down his very hard, very happy body. It doesn't help my rasping breaths or blazing cheeks. He smirks, unruffled.

The bastard.

"Semi-indestructible," I say, my chin in the air.

The congregation settles behind us. Steph's smirk rivals Hunter's.

Thank goodness I banned all media attendance, and not just because I'm sick of being lauded as the leader of humanity's rebellion against the Protectorate. I'm no leader. I stumbled on the victory weapon while clumsily trying not to die. If it weren't for Hunter, I would've spent the rest of the apocalypse in hiding until humanity inevitably lost.

Not exactly the brave and glorious rebel queen some outlets have depicted me as.

The priest clears his throat twice before he manages to speak. "Blessed be to God and our Holy Angels. The bride and groom will now join me in the sacristy with their two witnesses for the signing of the marriage licence."

We traipse down a short corridor to the side of the sanctuary and enter a small but ornate wood-panelled room, Steph and Dev trailing behind for a quick canoodle. Closets circle a wide desk, no doubt containing the vestments for mass and other paraphernalia like candles, bells and a wine decanter. A tiny, marble sink breaks the monotony of the wood.

Hunter carefully prints his name on the document on the priest's shiny desk. I sign next to him, followed by Steph and Dev, whose signature is a line that scours the paper.

He had no interest in learning to read and write alongside Hunter, whereas Hunter absorbed everything I taught him. He still loves it when I read to him, though. It's part of our bedtime routine.

"We will give you a moment alone to reflect on your sacred union." The priest shoos Steph and Dev into the corridor. "Please join us when you're ready to lead the procession to Newhailes."

We're having our reception in the conservatory of the grand estate house since we wouldn't all fit in the nook where Hunter and I spent the majority of the apocalypse. The conservatory has also been refurbished thanks to the surge in tourism.

The rustle of the priest's vestments disappears in Steph and Dev's wake, leaving the two of us—the silent and implacable Hunter, and me, the little quivering mouse who somehow captivated him. His breath brushes the top of my head, sending a skitter of goosebumps down my neck.

"Is reflect another word for sex?" he says.

I huff a laugh. "No. We're supposed to think about our marriage and the big commitment we've made."

"I read a book on weddings." Hunter nuzzles my ear. "It had a word I liked."

"What word?"

"Consummate," he purrs.

At my hitch of breath, he hoists me onto the edge of the desk and gathers the intricate material of my dress in one hand, exposing me to the waist through the split in the side. My heels are strappy and white, the laces criss-crossing up my calves. Hunter runs a fingertip across my tulle panties, tracing the pattern of golden leaves. His thighs spread my knees, and his thumb dips lower.

"We can't," I gasp. Despite the words, my pelvis tilts, begging for more of his clever fingers. "The priest could come…"

Hunter swallows my feeble protest. One tug frees my underwear, and he slides it off my legs.

"Then we will have to be fast"—he nips at my throat—"*wife.*"

I groan, scrabbling at the ties of his trousers. He palms my arse in one hand to easily hold me in position, then hesitates, one thrust away from further desecrating the church.

"I will not hurt?"

"Nope," I pant. "You won't hurt me."

Hunter has no problems in the size department. Hunter is *fucking scary* in the size department. But he never hurts me. He gets to be gentle. He gets to love and be loved.

His quick grin dissolves my insides. He eases between my legs to stretch me tight and full. I whimper but he doesn't pause until he's buried to the hilt. He's used to the many noises he draws from me and can tell the difference between pleasure and pain.

With the Creators, he knew only pain.

He rocks between my legs, stroking every part of me with the electrifying burn of his invasion. Tingles skate up my thighs and coil heat in my core. I drive my hips to meet him, and his breathing gets choppy. The whisper of my name on his lips is the only prayer I need. I shatter beneath the heavy surge of climax, boneless and intoxicated. Hunter cries out, the flex of his body launching me higher. He collapses over me, propped on his hands, his wings arched and fluttering. A fallen angel captured and tamed.

The glow of the orgasm has barely dimmed before glass shatters out in the nave. Steph screams.

And then there's the awful, haunting song of an arrow.

2

I pull my underwear on so fast, I give myself a wedgie. I hop off the priest's defiled desk but Hunter corrals me behind his towering frame before I can sprint down the corridor in my dress and heels, shrieking for Steph.

More screaming from the nave. More singing.

Knives appear in Hunter's hands, because of course his wedding outfit includes weapons. He'll have at least four others magically stuck to his person. I suspect he might be magnetic, though it's never been proven.

"Stay here, Maia," he says.

"Hunter…" My voice wobbles. "You know I can't do that."

He nods. "Then keep behind me."

He holds out a knife and I take it, squeezing it in my sweaty hand. He draws another from under his shirt. They're all specially made with a high iron content. The angels' only weakness.

Hunter stalks into the corridor towards the sound of battle, unperturbed like the warrior he is. I scuttle in his wake, struggling to breathe past my heartbeat.

Chaos greets us in the nave. Wings churn in the air above broken wood, jewel-toned battering against white-gold. Arrows howl through shattered glass, their tips and shafts swirling a soul-sucking blue. A pile of dusty vestments behind the lectern marks the remains of the priest. Angel fights angel in terrifying silence while the invited residents of Martello Court cower behind pillar and pew. More white- and golden-winged creatures spill through the windows and the obliterated double door into the antechamber.

The Protectorate have returned.

What a fool I am, thinking we were safe. We've come a long way in sustainable living and green energy since the Creators' punishment—siccing their creations on us to almost dust half of the population. I knew they'd return to claim their rebellious property but I thought we'd have more time. I thought we'd be ready.

And I never thought it would happen on my goddamn wedding day.

Hunter and I crouch in the shadows at the end of the corridor, my gaze darting over the melee. Between the far edge of the pews, I glimpse Dad's skinny, beige-clad behind as he arches his body like a caterpillar's and slithers across broken glass in the aisle formed by the pillars, disappearing through the archway to the chapel.

If he hides in there, he should be okay. I can't reach him yet. Not with the mass of angels separating us.

My heart leaps at a flash of sapphire. Devinon streaks above the pews, Steph and Greg tucked in each armpit. Steph has lost her wig, her brown hair in disarray from her short ponytail.

She's always hated her natural colour, even when she grew it out after her transition. She said it was uninspiring, unlike the woman she was born to be.

A flurry of arrows thuds into Dev's back. His flight falters. He drops his precious cargo on the steps to the sanctuary and collides with the lectern, tumbling into the altar behind it. Ceremonial candlesticks and a golden chalice clang to the floor. He lies still, weakened by the sickening pull of the arrows, though they can't kill him. The dust of the priest powders his suit.

Steph yells his name and crawls towards him, her cane nowhere to be seen in the carnage of feathers. No splashes of silver blood brighten the tainted beauty of the church. Greg grabs Steph's bicep and hauls her upright. Together they stagger to the crumpled Devinon. Three angels break from the group swirling above the nave, aiming for them.

And not the good kind of angel.

Hunter moves at the same time I do. He bounds into the air, his huge, black wings snapping wide. I skid onto the sanctuary, flashing a lot of thigh and planting myself in front of Steph and Greg's unprotected backs, brandishing my knife. Hunter ploughs into the three angels. His blade slashes. Liquid silver arcs, and patters on the hem of my dress. A corpse thuds onto the steps, white-gold wings awry. The head bounces under a pew. The long, copper hair tangles around the kneeler cushions. It reminds me of another red-haired angel who lost her head on the snowy esplanade of Edinburgh Castle.

Persipha. The bitch.

The two remaining angels parry Hunter's blows with their swords, milky-yellow froth stippling their arms and chests. I retreat to where Steph and Greg huddle over a groaning Devinon, my eyes on the battle.

Arrows bristle from the bodies in the pews, wings of emerald and ruby and violet ruffled and broken. A group of five are subdued on their knees, their flesh parted in horrible, bloodless wounds. Their super-sealing ability means their injuries clot instantly unless iron is involved.

Then they bleed.

A glance at Hunter confirms he's holding his own. One angel's arm hangs useless, the other's chest a wash of silver and sickly bubbles. Hunter's shirt is ripped at the sleeves and missing a few buttons. He swipes at a wailing arrow and sends it clattering into a pillar.

He never won the dominance fights encouraged by his savage culture and his equally savage creators. They weren't permitted to kill but, since they could heal quickly, they were allowed to hurt each other. Hunter was tired of hurting. He was lonely. He just wanted to be gentle.

Now, he can kill. Now, he has a reason to win beyond forcing himself on the loser.

My gentle angel slams his blade into the heart of his opponent, and twists. Silver gouts over his hand. The warrior drops into the pews in a snap of wood. Hunter lunges for the remaining angel.

"So much for our early-warning system," Steph mutters.

I sidle around until I'm on the other side of Dev, facing outwards so I can keep watch on Hunter. The rest of the Protectorate squadron or unit or whatever they call themselves are still preoccupied with cowing our angels—the Jewels of the Protectorate, as we have affectionately nicknamed them. The Martello Court residents lob pieces of broken furniture to distract and annoy since we all made the mistake of not carrying our weapons to a wedding.

"The Global Protection Alliance did mention it was in the testing phase," I say.

Greg snorts. "I bet the Creators had no trouble bypassing it. They are the 'most advanced race' and the 'first intelligent life'." He makes air quotes with his fingers. "This is bullshit, man. Why can't they leave us alone?"

"Fucking arseholes," Steph spits.

She grabs an arrow, grimaces, and yanks it from Devinon's back. I force my fingers around a slick, cold shaft. Even though I'm braced for the freezing jolt, my stomach rolls, threatening to spill my guts all over the sprawled Dev. Greg flings an arrow under the altar. Our background chorus is the frantic flap of wings, grunts and the smack of flesh on flesh. Sirens howl, distant but coming.

I hope they bring a shit-tonne of iron.

Dev cracks open one sapphire eye. His fingers creep across the floor to clutch at Steph's knee.

"You must flee, my delicate butterfly," he croaks.

I catch Greg mid eye-roll and he ducks his head. His cheeks flare pink.

"You must run and save yourselves." Dev sweeps us all out of his one eye. "We have lost."

"Maia," Hunter says in the sudden, echoing silence.

My head snaps up. His back is to us, his wings curled protectively, arms spread and knives pointed down. Tension ripples across his shoulders. In the mess of the nave beyond, every gem-winged angel is down, either pinioned by the Protectorate or limp from the effect of multiple arrows.

The only humans left unmolested are me, Steph and Greg. And hopefully my dad, still cloistered in the chapel. The Martello Court residents are on their knees, glowing blue arrows pressed to their throats.

I swallow hard, fighting a rush of bile. My fingers clamp on my knife. Hunter faces an unbroken line of white- and golden-winged angels. Their expressions are empty, though their eyes are filled with violence.

"Leave the humans unharmed and I will return without a fight," Hunter says.

"No, Hunter!" I yelp.

He twitches, a tiny movement, but doesn't turn around. "I promised to protect you. If I have to leave to keep you safe, then I will."

"But—"

"Maia," he says, soft and low, "remember—forever and always."

A sob lodges in my throat. Hot tears burn my cheeks and dapple my dress.

An angel barges through the line to stand alone in front of Hunter. Sunflower-yellow hair, the same colour as one of Steph's wigs, falls to his waist. His eyes are a sooty grey that emphasises the black hole of his pupils. All warrior angels are muscled but this one is twice as wide as the rest.

"You think to bargain, *Hunter?*" the hulking angel sneers. "Your pet human and her two insurgents will be coming with us."

Hunter slides his foot backwards, widening his stance. "Then we will fight, *Uziyah.*"

A chilling smile rewards Hunter's defiance. Uziyah crosses his arms over his bare chest. Loose trousers flow to his equally bare feet, a cloth belt knotted at his hip.

"You will come quietly or we will reduce every human in here to dust, and still take the ones we want. But for every minute you have delayed me, I will slice a finger from your little *ishansalla.*"

My knowledge of Hunter's language may be rudimentary but, going by his growl, the word isn't an endearment.

"Maia?" His voice asks everything he can't say out loud.

He will fight them, all of them, and kill as many as he can before they maim him into unconsciousness. He may save some of the Martello Court residents but most of them will crumble to dust from the pierce of an arrow at their throats. Maybe Uziyah will slide Hunter's iron knife into his heart for all the trouble he's caused, expensive commodity of the Creators or no. We'll still be kidnapped. The choice is whether it's in one piece, or several. Though there really is no choice, not if it risks Hunter or my friends.

"Don't," I whisper.

His wings droop. The sight of it is a kick in the stomach. A sign of defeat he hasn't shown since he escaped the Creators' grasp.

But their reach is long, and unforgiving.

Hunter's knives clatter to the floor.

3

"As I thought," Uziyah says, his sneer wrinkling his mouth. "You are a traitor and a coward."

The handle of the knife bites into my palm. Devinon struggles to push himself up at my feet. Steph and Greg dart in to assist, supporting the angel under each arm. Greg barely reaches his chest.

I wish I could see Hunter's face.

"You bested me before, Uziyah," Hunter says softly. "But challenge me now and the outcome will be different."

The warriors stare at each other, Hunter slightly elevated by his position on the top step of the sanctuary. Outside, the sirens reach a crescendo then squawk into silence. Tyres screech through the shattered, stained-glass windows. Doors slam. The lack of singing arrows and screams hopefully mean there are no more angels outside the church.

Each country has their own Warrior Angel Counter Offensive team (or WACO team for short), trained by the GPA. If an angel has white or golden wings, they'll shoot it on sight. We were caught out by religious fervour and awe when the Protectorate first appeared—until they stabbed the Pope, of course—but we know what they are now. We know how to fight them.

Uziyah wraps a hand around the pommel of the sword at his hip. "Our challenge will have to wait. Your little rebellion is over. You and the other traitors will be judged by your betters on the ship."

He mounts the stairs. Hunter tenses but stays still while Uziyah runs his blocky fingers over him. Material rips under his rough touch.

"No, Maia," Hunter says without turning around, catching me mid-step.

A knife clatters to the floor. Four more are pulled from his boots, and discarded.

Uziyah's smile chills me to my strappy shoes. "I will carry your human myself."

"You will not touch her," Hunter growls.

Uziyah chuckles. "Enjoy your defiance while it lasts, *moally tumsasha.*"

He moves to circle past Hunter but Hunter retreats, fists clenched, keeping his body between me and the advancing angel. I touch Hunter's warm back, bracketed by the softness of his wings and his comforting smell of ice. Tension vibrates beneath my palm. Shielded from sight, I slip my knife into his boot since my wedding dress wasn't made for concealing weaponry.

Steph makes a noise of protest, joined by a huff from Greg. I peek around Hunter's wing. Uziyah wraps Steph and Greg in his bulging arms, squashing them into immobility. Devinon wobbles, unsupported, but before he can collapse, another warrior swoops in and grabs him. Throughout the church, the rest of our angels are manhandled by the Protectorate. The Martello Court residents are shoved on their faces. I do a quick count, the worry in my chest easing when I reach ten.

Uziyah barks a word in his language.

"We are here for retribution, not slaughter—as much as you deserve it." Uziyah sneers at Hunter. "Follow or it will become the latter."

He hops off the sanctuary and marches down the central aisle, a wriggling, cursing Steph and Greg trapped in his hold. Greg's hair has pulled free and sticks to the sweat on his face. He shoots me a wide-eyed look of terror over Uziyah's meaty shoulder. Hunter scoops me against his chest, exactly how a groom should carry his bride on their wedding day, though it's usually across a threshold for wedding night fun, not so we can follow our friends as we all get kidnapped right off the face of the freaking Earth. We stalk in Uziyah's wake past rows and rows of the Protectorate and their captives and the Martello Court residents huddled at their feet. As soon as we pass them, the warriors close in behind us, dragging their prisoners and leaving the humans sprawled on the floor.

"He's kind of a dick, isn't he?" I whisper.

"Yes," Hunter says, "he is."

He sounds as implacable as always, whereas my pulse quivers through my voice.

We managed to survive the apocalypse on our planet; how are we supposed to survive a whole bunch of pissed-off angels in space? Not to mention their probably more pissed-off creators?

"I don't want to go to your ship," I mumble.

A beat of silence then, "Neither do I."

The Protectorate are all about domination. Dominating the universes they're sent to punish, dominating each other. Hunter suffered numerous cruelties to abide by the rules of his twisted culture. Now they're forcing him to go back. What will they do to him? What will they do to *us?*

The WACO team better be more effective than our bloody warning system.

I strain to peer over Hunter's shoulder and beyond the unflinching army herding us to our doom. Sunlight spills through the broken door as we approach, the contrast darkening the inside of the church. I glimpse a wisp of hair and a pale face peeking around the archway into the chapel. A burst of relief eclipses the panic and helplessness churning in my stomach.

My dad will be okay. A small mercy.

I wonder if I'll ever see him again.

Other cautious faces peer over the pews. More relief. Knowing the cruelty of angels, I half-expected them to dust the rest of my wedding guests out of spite.

Steph bleats my name. My head whips around. Uziyah launches himself through the door of the church. Sunlight gilds the gold in his feathers.

"Hold on, Maia," Hunter says.

His grip tightens. I throw my arms around his neck and hug him hard. His wings snap wide then he leaps out the door into nothing but blazing white and the scent of fresh, spring air. I squint against the brightness.

Black and boxy vehicles block the street beyond the narrow car park. Soldiers hunker behind the barricades that swing from the sides like stunted wings. No gawkers stand on the pavements. Not even a curtain twitch from a nearby house.

The Protectorate already taught us how to hide.

We gain height, zooming towards the WACO team. I steel myself for the clatter of gunfire. Wind tugs at my hair and slithers under the thin material of my dress, flapping it around my calves. The *thwup-thwup-thwup* of a helicopter battles the thud of Hunter's heart and mine.

We flash over the rooftops without a single shot being fired. Again, I strain to see past Hunter's shoulder and the flap of his wings as his muscles power us after Uziyah. Gem-winged angels form a fleshy shield, clutched to the chests of their captors.

Relying on human sentimentality to shield them—the Protectorate have planned this well.

Even without the Order of the Holy Angels, our Jewels have become a part of our society. They helped us rebuild, shared the secrets of clean, Creator technology. They came to our world from a culture of pain and dominance but they stayed for the freedom.

Finally, a burst of gunfire. An angel shudders in mid-air, her arms empty since we're outnumbered. Silver blood glitters in the sunlight. She looses a wailing arrow downward, my view blocked by roofs as we continue to gain height. Four more creatures draw their bows. Feathers puff from the ruined wings of the bullet-pocked warrior. She drops from sight, joined by another. The rest dodge and fly faster, clearing the roof.

The ground dwindles. The helicopter reduces another angel without a living shield to a spiralling body.

Thank all the gods for iron. Without it, the Protectorate could take the damage and keep on ticking.

Vertigo tugs at my gut. Higher we go. Higher still. An arrow pierces the cabin of the pursuing helicopter. The vehicle jerks sideways then nosedives, rotors spinning. It dwindles to a speck lost amongst the green and brown and grey of the land far below. I shudder in Hunter's grip despite his body temperature, deafened by the flap of many wings and the whoosh of wind.

"I will keep you safe, Maia," he says in my ear.

I relax my arms a tiny bit and press my cold cheek to his warm one.

"I'll keep *you* safe," I say.

He turns his head further, and his lips brush mine. I kiss him back, frantic, my hair whipping around us. Fear threatens to steal my breath more than the chill air and the altitude.

"Jesus, man, is that a UFO?" Greg yells.

In the blue vastness above us, something shimmers—a reflective surface rippling like a pool disturbed by a stone. It appears to be about the size of a double-decker bus, though ovoid.

Can it be called a UFO if we already know what it is?

"It's a lot smaller than I imagined," I struggle to say past my chattering teeth.

"That is not the spaceship," Hunter says. "It is the shuttle that will take us there. Even we cannot survive in a vacuum."

I tremble in Hunter's arms. The air is difficult to breathe. Thin and freezing.

What if we can't breathe on their ship? Is that our punishment—to have us die, gasping, on the floor at their feet? Or do the Creators have something worse planned for us?

A black opening yawns wide in the side of the shuttle. Uziyah streaks towards it and disappears into the darkness.

4

The interior of the shuttle is like being in a mirror maze. Everything is a confusion of reflections and glass. The transparent material of the outer wall affords a view of endless blue sky. The shiny black floor sparkles as if constellations are trapped in it. A sucking noise signals the closing of the door.

Uziyah shoves Steph and Greg away from him. They bounce off the wall and stumble further down the corridor. Greg manages to slot his shoulder under Steph's arm before they end up on the ground.

Funny, I've never noticed how much shorter Greg is compared to Steph.

"Arsehole," Steph hisses, glaring at Uziyah.

If she had her cane, she'd be in his face, poking a manicured nail into his pec and calling him a fruit fly.

She should've been the leader of the resistance, not me. She's fearless and feisty. I can barely keep it together. Most days, I forget to brush my hair. This is as dishevelled as I've ever seen her—wig gone, make-up smudged—and we lived through the apocalypse.

Hunter lowers my feet to the ground, and I slink around Uziyah's bulk. Uziyah's eyes follow me, dilated yet pale in the weirdly dim and shifting light of the craft. My wedding dress whispers like the wings of angels. A clunk ripples in the soles of my shoes.

"What the hell was—"

A force slams me to the ground in a tangle with Steph and Greg. An elbow digs into my ribs. Or maybe a knee. The Protectorate and their captured warriors sway a bit but remain standing. I struggle against an invisible weight pressing me down. Hunter stoops over me, his wings eclipsing the sky. The roof is no longer blue, but black and roiling with clouds. Dizziness swoops through my gut the longer I stare at it.

Hunter peels me off the floor. "I am sorry, Maia. I did not think of the acceleration affecting you. You will adjust to the sensation."

"We're *moving?*" I gasp.

My fingers grip his forearms. I twist to gape out the side of the shuttle. There's nothing but more blackness and boiling grey.

"You will not be able to see beyond the distortion," Hunter says.

"But where is—"

"Little help here?" Greg groans from the floor.

Hunter props me against the wall, then again when my body tries to keel over. Heaviness fills my limbs with sand, everything an effort. I widen my stance to keep myself from face-planting.

"*Ishansalla,*" Uziyah says, sneering at me.

Hunter bares his teeth, and crouches beside Steph and Greg. He drags them vertical. They manage to hold each other up, though their legs quiver.

Uziyah draws his sword, the eerie blue reflecting off every surface. Coldness wafts from the blade in the close confines of the shuttle. My skin goosebumps and attempts to crawl away.

"Walk," he says, "if you can even do that."

Steph and Greg stagger a few steps, Greg's arm clamped around Steph's waist to take most of her weight. I clutch Hunter and force my legs to move. My heels scrape the floor.

"Christ"—Steph winces—"it's like someone's using all my nerves as a swing."

Greg jerks his head to look over his shoulder at Hunter. "How fast are we accelerating if this is what it feels like?"

"Fast," Hunter says.

We shuffle down the corridor followed by the silence of angels. Soft rustles betray their presence. The occasional groan from one of our injured. A door slides open on our left, leading deeper into the craft.

"Get in," Uziyah barks.

Steph and Greg tumble through. Hunter hoists me inside. The rest of the Protectorate and their prisoners stream past in the corridor behind Uziyah, pausing only to shove Devinon across the threshold. He sprawls on his front, sapphire wings akimbo. The pins on his suit jacket and shirt have ripped free, the slits in the material giving glimpses of his muscled back.

"The Creators look forward to welcoming you home properly, Hunter," Uziyah says with one of his chilling smiles. "As do I."

The door glides shut, a hiss of locks sealing us into a room with more reflections and black, cloudy sky. Steph and Greg sink down beside Devinon and get him sitting against the wall, his legs stretched out. His colour looks better, less sickly. He tucks an arm around Steph and pulls her into his side. Greg hugs his knees, squashing himself into the corner to avoid leaning on Dev's wing. His suit is scuffed at the elbows.

"Come here, Gregory," Dev says tiredly.

Greg hunches tighter around his knees. "It's Greg, not Gregory."

"Your full name is Gregory Coltrain."

"People call me Greg."

"Come here, Greg," Dev says, "unless you want a nickname like my delicate butterfly? You could be my prickly pear."

Greg rolls his eyes but scoots the couple of feet separating him from the angel.

"I'm not your anything," he huffs. "And I don't need a hug."

Dev manages a half-smile. "Maybe I need a hug."

The surreality of the moment—of *everything*—threatens to crumple me to the floor. I hobble to the wall and press my hands to the glass, though it's not glass. It's pliant but strong, with a whole lot of cloudy nothingness beyond.

"Why can't I see anything?" I say. "Where's Earth? Where are *we?*"

Gentle hands cup my shoulders. I lean into the firm, warm chest instead of panting condensation onto the window. Viewing portal. *Whatever.*

"We are travelling in a pocket of distorted space. It enables us to move faster than the speed of light." Hunter pauses, sliding his arms around me, his hands splayed on my belly. "Our ship will be at the furthest reaches of your solar system."

"What are we talking here?" Greg pipes up. "The Oort Cloud?"

"The what now?"

I sway in Hunter's arms. My body feels both heavy and light, my brain a buzz of static. I desperately try to pick out something familiar in the swirling grey of distorted space, and almost laugh.

There's nothing familiar out here. I'm in freaking *space*.

"Come, Maia. Sit."

Hunter reverses until his back hits the wall opposite Steph, Greg and Devinon. He slides down, cradling me in his lap. His wings tickle my arms and blanket me in a soft cocoon. I twirl his wedding ring on his slim finger, unable to stop. Round and around.

"This can't be happening," I blurt, hating how high my voice is. "A second ago, we were married and having se—I mean, contemplating our sacred union. In the priest's office. Now we're here. On a spaceship to another spaceship. Kidnapped by angels."

My voice rises in decibel and volume. My ribs heave against the constriction of Hunter's arms. He nuzzles my hair and cuddles me tighter.

"We will get through this," he says, his warm breath stroking my ear. "I will not let them ruin what we have built."

Steph blinks somewhat glassy eyes.

"Wait a minute." She scrubs her face and smears her make-up worse, but some pink returns to her cheeks. "Did you just say you had sex? In the priest's *office?*"

I clear my throat. "Uh, on his desk actually."

She gives me a wide grin. It's slightly demented but it eases the anxiety stabbing at my chest.

"You dirty, glorious bastard," she breathes.

Greg splutters.

Dev scrunches his brow and says, "Is a bastard good?"

I laugh until my stomach hurts and the only thing holding me up is Hunter wrapped around me. Steph and Greg giggle into Dev's chest. I hiccup, loudly, and it sets us off again until I'm wheezing and blinded by tears, but a little calmer.

Nothing like a semi-hysterical fit to clear the sinuses.

"Humans are strange," Dev says.

Hunter places a tender kiss on the top of my head. "Yes, they are."

"Sorry, I needed that." I hiccup again. "This is all a bit… overwhelming. You two may be fine with zooming across time and space but I've never even left Scotland, never mind Planet Earth."

"I really need a vape," Greg sighs.

Steph and I share a chuckle, but sober quickly.

I tilt my head to look at Hunter. "What does *ishansalla* mean?"

He shifts underneath me.

"Feeble creature," he finally says.

"Well, it wasn't any worse than what I was imagining. What about the other one—*moally* something?"

He smirks, his eyes dark above the jut of his cheekbones. "It translates to 'couples with humans.'"

Greg snorts. "Aww, human fucker and angel fucker. You're a complete set."

"I thought we agreed my call sign was Angeltamer," I say through my teeth.

"You agreed," Greg sniffs. "My suggestion was better."

"What do you think they're going to do—the Creators?" Steph picks at a loose thread in the seam of her dress, the silk creased.

I shrug one shoulder, feigning nonchalance. "If they wanted to kill us, they would have done it on Earth. They spared everyone, which is unusual for them. They didn't complete their cull but we've learned our lesson—we've reversed a lot of damage since the Protectorate left. They can't say our universe is a threat to the others anymore."

"They will not accept the defeat, nor our insubordination, without punishment," Hunter says.

"Maybe they just need to get over themselves," I mutter.

I snuggle closer to Hunter, tangling my fingers in his and pressing our rings together.

We should be at Newhailes right now, dancing in the conservatory and stuffing ourselves with cake. When everyone was distracted by the antics of easily inebriated angels, we would have snuck away to the security room—our nook where we kept each other safe during the apocalypse and where we did… other things. Other things I'd planned on repeating while everyone else partied downstairs.

A hush falls over our cell in the alien shuttle, the light constantly shifting, swirling. The reflections and refractions give me a headache. Staring out the window makes me want to throw up.

I still can't believe we're in space. *Outer* space. The vacuum between planets and stars. Flying deeper and deeper, where no human has ever been, where our most powerful telescopes have barely penetrated. No one can follow us out here. We're completely, utterly alone and surrounded by enemies.

I read somewhere that it would take almost two years at the speed of light to reach the edge of our solar system. Hunter says we're travelling faster than that but how much faster? Will we get there in a year? Eight months? Hunter and Dev aren't acting like we'll be stuck in this room for months. Is this the same route they took when they first attacked us?

"How long," I croak, then try again. "How long to reach your ship?"

Hunter has a silent conversation with Devinon over my head.

Warrior angels can convey a lot with just their eyeballs.

"Six human months," he finally says.

"Six months! They're going to keep us locked up like this for *six months?*"

"No." Hunter tucks a curl of hair behind my ear, my fancy up-do completely trashed. "We will sleep through it."

"Sleep?"

"Come. I will show you."

He urges me to my feet and faces the wall we were leaning on. His palm splays on a section that looks no different to the rest of the strange, swirling material—except for my bemused reflection staring back at me. A double panel retracts to reveal a row of eight vertical tubes. Something pink and squidgy-looking fills the rear of each.

"We're supposed to sleep in there?" I say, my mouth dry.

"It is not so bad. It feels like you close your eyes for only a moment, no matter how long the journey."

"Hold up," Greg says, suddenly reanimated. "Is this cryosleep?"

"I do not know that word."

"Like, we get in there and it freezes us so we can travel for billions of light years without ageing?"

Greg jumps to his feet, wobbles, and joins us at the wall compartment, running his hands over a tube. The front hisses open. He jerks back with a surprised laugh.

"Not frozen," Hunter says. "But, yes—a form of stasis."

"Will it work on us despite our different body chemistry and metabolism?"

"The pods are capable of sustaining any biological organism. The Creators use this technology to transport creatures between universes."

"What happens when we get to this Ooh Cloud place?" I say, eyeing the pink goo and glass pods warily.

"Ooh Cloud," Greg snickers. "You're so uneducated, Maia."

"Shut up, Greg," I say.

"We will cross to our universe," Hunter says, ignoring Greg. "The journey is instantaneous."

"Woah." Greg places a hand on his chest as if he might swoon. "Are we talking wormholes now?"

Hunter cocks his head. "Worms are the little creatures that burrow in your soil. I do not understand the connection."

"A wormhole is a tunnel through space-time that could, hypothetically, be used to cross galaxies."

"We are crossing much further than galaxies."

"Universes, whatever. But is it a wormhole?"

"If that is also a portal and a ripple in space-time then, yes, we are talking wormholes now."

Greg bounces on his toes. "Fucking hyper-drive, cryosleep and wormholes? This is so cool."

Steph appears at his shoulder and slaps the back of his head. "Cool? None of this is cool, you idiot."

"I was trying to lighten the mood." Greg pouts and rubs his skull. "Unless you want to talk about how screwed we are? Because that's fucking depressing."

Damn. The sci-fi babble *was* soothing my jangling nerves, the adrenaline leaching away. But now I remember I have no phone, no food. Just my wedding dress and shoes, and the ring on my finger. An iron knife that's more effective in Hunter's hands than mine. Perhaps I can poke a Creator in the eye with one of my hairpins. The few that weren't scattered to the winds on the flight to the shuttle, anyway.

The cloudy nothingness swirls beyond the window. A

metallic scrape startles me. Steph and Greg jump but the implacable Hunter is unmoved. Devinon crouches beside a smaller open panel at the end of the room. Eight cylindrical containers pop out on some kind of rack. Liquid sloshes, turbid and beige.

"That's not the dinner I ordered." I cross my arms. "We should be having maple-glazed pork, seared asparagus and mashed potatoes not... *that.*"

Dev hands us each a jar, slotting himself in the middle of Steph and Greg. I unscrew the lid and sniff the contents suspiciously, just like Hunter used to whenever I gave him something he was unfamiliar with. The liquid smells like bubblegum and mud.

Hunter swallows the mixture in three gulps. "It is not unpleasant."

Dev copies him, licking his lips and tossing the empty container perfectly into the rack without moving from his position sandwiched between Steph and Greg.

Bloody warrior angels. They're all a bunch of show-offs.

"Could it poison us?" I sniff the liquid a second time. "Same point on the metabolism and body chemistry."

"It contains basic nutrients—proteins and sugars—so it should not. But start slow. Like when you painted my wing." Hunter gives me a secret smile.

Steph smirks. "I remember that day. It was so cute how worried you were over a bit of chalk."

I wrinkle my nose at her, then take an experimental sip. My face attempts to collapse in on itself.

"Holy mother, that's tart," I gasp.

Steph and Greg take their own spluttering sips. We wait for our insides to shrivel or our skin to swell but time passes unmarked and the shuttle shuttles onward. I drink a third of the container, my belly already bloated.

"Gah." I smack my lips. "I can't drink anymore."

Hunter takes the flask from my hands and returns it to the rack. "You are tiny. That should be enough."

Steph smirks at me and relinquishes her own gloopy leftovers to Devinon. We turn back to the stasis pods.

"We should sleep now," Dev says.

My pulse flutters uncomfortably. Hunter pulls me into his arms.

"You will be safe. I will be here when you wake."

"Are you sure?" I whisper into his chest.

He kisses me softly. "I am sure."

He guides me into the nearest tube. My back settles into warm, squidgy goo. Claustrophobia claws at my guts but to distract myself, I watch Steph enter the pod next to mine. Dev hugs a squirming Greg then slots him into a tube out of my sight on the other side of Steph. Hunter flicks his wings, and they brush the side of the glass on my right. I try to turn my head to look at him but the pink stuff cradles my skull, my nape. It thickens somehow, inching up to cover my limbs and tickle my sides. A whimper escapes me.

"Breathe, Maia," Hunter says.

I gulp in air, still tasting the tartness of the drink and smelling something like oranges. My heart slams against my ribs and echoes off the narrow walls of the chamber.

The transparent door glides shut.

The creeping slime weaves tendrils through my hair and across my cheeks. I can feel it when I blink.

The double panel closes us into the compartment. An amorphous blue-grey glow fills the space.

"I love you, Hunter," I say, the words loud in the tube, though there's a decent amount of room since it's built for the bulkiness of angels.

"I love you, too," he says, his voice muffled. "Sleep well, Maia."

I shut my eyes.

My last thought is swallowed by the goo before I can finish it.

5

Hunter wasn't wrong. It feels as if I've only just shut my eyes when he's shaking me carefully awake. It's like coming around from anaesthesia—his face appears down a long, black tunnel, getting closer, more distinct, until he's right in front of me. I blink at him. Dark hair falls into dark eyes.

"We are here," he says.

It's a lot more ominous than waking up at the dentist's after I got a couple of molars out.

I step into him and breathe his clean scent. "Are you sure it's been six months? I don't feel any different."

"Stasis, Maia," he says.

Devinon scoops Steph out of her tube and loops her arm in his for support. Greg yawns and stretches.

"That slime is weird shit, man."

I check but there's not a hint of goo left on my skin. No residue, no stickiness. Did it slide into my mouth and nose while I slept? Is that how it works?

We drink another round of tart, beige glop from more beakers that pop out of the wall. The door to our cell hisses open and frames the bulk of Uziyah. A breeze stirs his sunflower-yellow hair. His hand tightens on the pommel of the sword at his hip.

"Out," he grunts. "Our creators are waiting."

Holy crap. We're going to meet the Creators. The civilisations that built the Protectorate to police the universes. Hunter described some of them as winged but less humanoid, whatever that means. They're technologically superior. Arrogant. Maybe a little terrifying.

I'm not exactly dressed for extrastellar diplomacy. Though I don't plan on being diplomatic. I have a few things to say about their so-called advanced race.

Uziyah spins on his heel and stalks down the corridor. We follow, herded again by the angels who crashed my wedding. The mass of white and gold drowns the wings of emerald and violet. I hustle after Uziyah, realising that the weighted sensation is gone. I drag my gaze from the sparkly floor, and all the air leaves my body in a rush. My knees lock. Hunter pauses one step beyond, cocking his head. Greg walks into my back with a quiet, "Oof."

"What the hell is that?" I squeak.

The cloudy distortion of faster-than-light travel has vanished from the transparent walls and roof of the shuttle. Blackness looms, speckled with stars. Except they're not stars—they're lights. Endless globes and streaks of them.

"Home," Hunter says grimly.

I asked him about the spaceship he came from. He said it was extremely big. This thing is *colossal*. We're too close to discern the broad shape of it, our tiny shuttle near the base, but it's dark and hulking and *alien*. It's all angles and lines, not smooth. Other shuttles like ours hang on either side of us, unconnected by anything I can see.

"You are testing my patience," Uziyah growls.

"You mean he actually has some?" Steph mutters behind me.

I turn my snort into a cough. Hunter smirks, his back to the impatient warrior.

"You'll have to excuse us poor *ishansallas*," I say, smiling sweetly. "We're basically tourists."

Uziyah narrows his eyes but stomps on without a word. He reaches the square door of the craft and seems to step out into nothing. He strides towards the spaceship without pause. I hesitate on the threshold, my fingers gripping the pliant wall. My shaking hand brushes the side of something solid beyond the doorway but it's more transparent than the windows and roof of the shuttle. Vertigo swoops into my stomach when I glance down into the void.

It feels like if I step out into it, I'll fall forever. Though if there were nothing separating me from the vastness of space, my eyeballs would've exploded by now.

Greg's shoulder bumps me. I yelp and stumble out of the shuttle. The ground is bouncy and there to catch me, even if I can't see it.

"Sorry, Maia," Greg says, not even looking at me. "That is the *Oort Cloud*," he breathes. "No human has ever seen this."

Greg can be annoying sometimes, and needs to be told to shut up a lot, but I'm glad he's here. Even in the midst of blood and disaster, he can find something funny or fascinating. The Creators might torture us in a few minutes but he's still geeking out over space stuff.

I hold my breath, and peek between my feet. The blackness grows misty past the bottom edge of the Protectorate ship. Chunks of rock—their scale difficult to determine—drift lazily, or spin. Some appear stationary. Deeper and deeper, they become infinite dots and clouds. Endless and everywhere. Surrounding us.

"So we were right about this place? It's really made of dormant comets and ice?"

"Who are you asking here, Greg?" I say.

"Not only comets and ice," Hunter says. "Pieces of planets. Broken moons. The waste of your universe. It is like a still pool on the edge of a river—detritus collects."

Greg raises his brows. "That's the most I've ever heard you speak."

"Just because you do not hear, does not mean I do not speak."

Greg's forehead crinkles. I grab his shirt and yank him into the docking corridor. His shriek causes Uziyah's sneer to deepen where he's standing inside the spaceship, glowering at us.

"Hunter means he saves his words for me, his wife, not you, the irritating friend of his wife."

I prod Greg until he staggers ahead.

"I don't think he meant the name-calling part," Greg mutters.

"So I embellished a little."

"I do not find you irritating, Greg," Devinon calls as we all shuffle into the invisible death trap. "You are prickly but sweet, like the pear."

Greg shoves his hands in his suit trousers, his shoulders hunched. The tips of his ears blush pink.

"For god's sake, Dev. We don't even have prickly pears in Scotland. How would you even know?"

"I tried one when I was in the country you call Mexico. It was spiny and interesting. Like you."

I smirk at Greg. "Is he flirting with you?"

"Shut up," he grunts, his shoulders around his ears. "He's not—"

"*Silence!*" Uziyah roars, and we all jump. All of us who bleed red, anyway. "There will be no more talking. This is not a human vacation. You are here to be *punished*. You will feel nothing but fear and regret."

"We are afraid." I wrap my fingers in Hunter's, and he squeezes my hand. "Maybe this is how we deal with it."

"Do not *deal* with it," Uziyah spits. "Suffer and bemoan your fate."

He marches into the Protectorate ship. The other angels press in, herding us onwards. We step inside a long corridor wide enough for two warriors to walk abreast. I was anticipating blackness and gloom to match the exterior but the walls are pearly and shining. The floor is a gleaming path of turquoise.

It's... pretty. Not what I expected given the brutality of angels and their culture of dominance. But I guess they didn't build it, the Creators did, and the Creators love their aesthetics.

The corridor splits into two arcs, one curving down and out of sight, the other curving up.

"Take those two with the rest," Uziyah barks. "Leave Devinon, Hunter and his *ishansalla*."

Steph squawks as she's ripped from Dev's arm and bundled into the grasp of a golden-winged angel. Dev reaches for her but two warriors slam him against the wall, a forearm across his throat. Uziyah draws his sword, pressing the tip to Dev's side and slicing the charcoal material of his already ruined suit.

"Fight, and I will slide this blade between your ribs until you are too sick to walk. Then I will dust your *ishansalla* for your insolence."

Steph kicks in her captor's arms, though it makes her wince. She's lost a shoe somewhere.

"I'll give *you* feeble, you steroidal hummingbird," she snarls.

Uziyah turns his glare on Greg, his sword steady on Dev's chest. My hand tightens in Hunter's. He swipes his thumb over my knuckles. Greg holds his hands up and sidles next to the wriggling Steph, nearly getting a toe in the eye. Dev watches, his expression stricken.

"Look after our delicate butterfly," he says.

Greg bites his lip but nods, his gaze downcast. The delicate butterfly in question claws at the forearms of the angel pinning her and tries to shatter his shin bone with her one remaining heel. A mass of bodies and feathers sweeps my two friends away. Steph twists in the angel's arms.

"Don't let them give you any shit, Maia," she pants. "They started this, not us."

"I won't. I'll see you soon," I croak, if only to convince myself.

Uziyah sheaths his sword and aims for the fork of the corridor that curves downward. Hunter and I fall into step behind him. The two angels pluck Devinon off the wall and shove him in our wake, prowling along at the rear.

The corridor spirals then flattens, the colours unchanging. More rounded and smooth passageways branch off. The sound of our footfalls is hushed, the air cool and smelling of metal. A low hum, so deep I feel it in my stomach, shivers through the walls and floor.

"We are moving for the portal," Hunter says quietly.

"No talking," Uziyah snaps.

The corridor widens into a grey, dome-shaped room, the apex coated in reflective silver. My eyes can't make sense of the two mirrored figures waiting for us. Screens filled with images of corridors and strange spaces and angels cover the remainder of the walls. The spread of Uziyah's golden wings blocks my view of the centre. The floor slopes upward towards a raised dais. Uziyah sweeps to the side.

And I get my first look at a Creator.

6

"Bloody hell, it's a dinosaur," I blurt.

Hunter shifts next to me, his hand in mine. His face has become the arrogant mask he wears when he's threatened but I'm an expert at his expressions now. Amusement sparks in his midnight-blue gaze.

"They can understand you, Maia," he says.

Well, crap.

Not that I'm going to apologise.

I tilt my chin and stare at the two creatures on the raised dais, the room gloomier than the bright corridors despite the many screens on the walls. Slashes of violet stare back, no pupil discernible at this distance. One creature clacks its beak to reveal pointed teeth. Scaled wings arch from their shoulders, their spines hunched, necks long. If they stood straighter, they'd be taller than the warrior angels, though their frames are all angles and bones.

Uziyah speaks in his language but I miss everything except for his favourite insult. One of the Creators moves in a bobbing, stalking gait, like a heron at the edge of a pond. The knee joints of its leg bend backwards. A tight bodysuit covers him—definitely a him—to his ankles, his bared skin as dark as his wings. The bony crest on the top of his skull is longer than the other Creator's by at least three inches.

Hunter, Dev and I watch him approach in our tattered wedding finery. The Creator stops in front of Hunter. The eyes narrow, and I finally see the tiny pin-prick of a pupil. The beak opens but no words spill out, only a disconcerting series of buzzes and clicks. He flicks his hand at me. He has two thumbs and four fingers and enough joints to make me think of a spider's leg.

Goosebumps prickle on my nape.

"What's he saying?" I meant to whisper but it comes out a little loud.

The buzzing increases in pitch, like a wasp trapped in a jar.

"He is telling me how disappointed he is in my disobedience," Hunter says with absolutely no inflection. "And he is insulting my wife."

I plant my fists on my hips and glare up at the Creator. "You want insults? How about you should be ashamed of yourselves for banging your own kids?"

More angry buzzing. The Creators' wings slither open and closed. Uziyah's face darkens but I keep talking before he can tell me how feeble I am.

"Sex, couple—whatever you want to call the mechanics of it. And, okay, they're not technically your kids—not biologically— but you built them. You *made* them. It is beyond creepy to think that entitles you to use their bodies however you wish."

The other Creator sweeps down the ramp and pads towards us. His wings are so large, they scrape on the floor like the hem of a cloak. Their voices vibrate in my ears. Long, articulated fingers reach for me.

"Do not dare," Hunter growls, shielding me with his arm.

The Creators pause. They share a wide, violet stare then

the hissing and clacking resumes, echoing in the dome of the ceiling.

"What a shame I can't understand you," I say, "because I haven't even mentioned the part where you encourage the warrior angels to hurt, dominate and rape each other. If you're surprised that some of them chose not to return, then you're not as intelligent as you think, no matter how advanced you are. We offered them a different life—one where they could love and be gentle."

Uziyah scoffs so hard, it's a wonder he doesn't choke. The Creators' wings flare and tangle since they're standing next to each other. They direct their buzzing to Uziyah. With a sharp nod, he strides from the room, glaring at me the whole way.

My heart rockets against my ribs. Nervousness wants me to keep babbling but I shut my mouth.

I can't believe I'm standing in a spaceship scolding an alien race. The weirdness of it threatens to leave me dizzy.

The Creators cease their hissing and watch us in silence, their heads moving to regard us from one slash of an eye then the other. They fold their hands in front of their hunched, sunken chests. Even their arms have an extra joint.

"Do they have names?" I whisper to Hunter, though there's no point in whispering.

"The first is Salam'ack'tai'moran. The other is Tallai'sig'chai. The longer their names, the elder they are. Salam'ack'tai'moran is the eldest on board."

"Would they be offended if I called them Salam and Tallai?"

A smirk flits across Hunter's lips. "Probably."

The Creators grumble. Wings flick in annoyance.

They both look the same to me—goodness, is that racist?

I squint. Salam's eyes are a brighter violet, almost neon.

Tallai is shorter. Their skin is dark grey, and pitted, though Tallai's is a shade lighter. The colour of wet ashes. Tallai has a sheen of purple in his wings when they catch the light from the corridor.

"Where's Uziyah gone?" I say to distract myself from their unblinking attention while they regard me with the patience of vultures.

"To get the healer," Hunter says.

"Why?" I squeak, imagining those beaks tearing into flesh. Spindly fingers crushing bone.

"They wish for your understanding. They do not like to be talked over. Or ignored."

I swallow. "How will—"

Uziyah returns, trailed by another Creator. She's wearing a mauve bodysuit unlike the darker versions of her brethren, who seem intent on sucking all the light and colour out of everything. It contains a belt filled with pouches. She folds her hands in front of her chest and bows to the two males, her skin a pale grey not unlike Uziyah's eyes. A short crest tops her bald head.

Does that mean she's younger? Hunter said Salam was the eldest and his crest sticks up like a shark's fin.

The Creators converse. Uziyah watches their huddle of three with calm reverence then switches his attention to ours and it morphs to a sneer.

"This is interesting," Devinon says quietly. "They are usually not so quick to share their advancements."

Hunter tilts his head to the angel behind his shoulder but keeps his gaze on the Creators. "It is an unprecedented time but you know them. They want their victims to understand exactly why they are being punished, otherwise how will they learn?"

"Uh, and what does—"

The female Creator swoops for me. I jerk to the side, slamming my shoulder into Hunter. He angles his chest to steady me, and his warm fingers circle my bicep.

"You do not need to struggle, Maia. It will not hurt."

"What won't?" I say.

"Technology."

My voice rises. "They're going to make me a cyborg, like you?"

"No, Maia," he says, flashing a brief grin. "Not quite like me."

As well as being semi-indestructible, Hunter and the rest of the warrior angels have wired technology in their brains to allow the instantaneous transfer of information on the civilisations they're about to infiltrate and punish. It also lets the Creators communicate with them and order them about. It was that call Hunter and our Jewels ignored when they chose to remain on Earth.

The female Creator hums at me, the noise not as grating as her male counterparts. Her eyes graduate from navy to amethyst nearer her beak, softening their stare. Diamonds of pale blue and pink decorate her wings. The nails on her splayed toes have been painted a matching colour.

Does that mean she's a little rebellious, choosing an alternative style to her peers? Salam and Tallai have no adornment but she's the only female I've seen so far. Maybe they all dress like that.

She cocks her head and slowly extends her arms, some kind of syringe gun in her hand. She makes what might be an enquiring sound.

I trust Hunter, so I suck in a breath and say, "Okay."

She gives me a chirp of encouragement, and hunches closer. She may be younger but she's still a similar height to the males glaring at me beyond the arch of her wings. Gentle hands cup my face and tilt my head to the side. Jointed fingers tuck my messy hair out of the way. A rubber nozzle settles in my ear. Cold liquid skooshes into the canal, crackling and bubbling. She repeats the process on my other ear. I flex my jaw to get my ears to pop. The muffled, full sensation slowly dissipates. The Creator tucks the syringe gun on a loop of her belt.

"So what was that for?" I say.

"Language comprehension. They do not wish to waste time with translation."

"Well, isn't that ni—wait a minute." I stare at the female. My hands fly to my ears. "I understood you! Holy crap, say something else."

The Creator dips her head. "What else would you like me to say, child?"

Her words come out clear over the buzzing and clicks of the original language still present as an undertone, the gunk in my ears translating it directly to something understandable. It's strange hearing it overlain together without any lag I can detect.

"Does this work on any language?"

"Yes, child, it—"

"You may leave, Bronwyn'challi," Salam snaps.

Bronwyn sweeps her wings and her body low then leaves the chamber. I shake myself, remembering I'm here because I've been abducted by a cruel, manipulative race who started the apocalypse, not to marvel and make friends.

Uziyah curls his lip. "Now you can understand when I call you a feeble creature, you feeble creature."

Again, I hear the angel's musical language underneath the mocking words.

"Enough, Uziyah," Salam says, and Uziyah falls silent, standing straighter. Salam paces closer. "It is your turn to listen, human—you and our wayward property."

I bristle but Hunter wraps his fingers around mine, pressing firmly.

"Your wasteful rebellion has cost us dear," Salam continues, the buzzing and clicking in the background like a fly battering itself against a window. "But it is done. We gave your line more leeway, less technological intervention, in the hope you would maintain the desired behaviours of your race at less expense. You have all been a disappointment. The recessive trait has already been expunged from the future generations we are being forced to build because of the stubbornness of humanity."

"*Our* stubbornness?" I blurt despite Hunter's soothing touch. "You sent an army to wipe out half our population. Did you think we'd simply lie down and take it?"

"It was a justified punishment for the negligence of your planet and the pollution of your universe."

I wave my free hand. "Look at all this technology you keep rubbing in our faces. Why didn't you help us? Why choose war and bloodshed?"

"You are a young and primitive civilisation. It is against universal law to share advanced knowledge with savage planets."

"But it's all right to slaughter us?" I snort. "Having better technology, or being an older race, doesn't make you more civilised, or should we go back to the part about you banging your creations and encouraging rape?"

Salam clicks his beak. "I am not here to debate with you, human. You have committed offences against our property and, by extension, our empire. You will receive your punishment with grace this time."

"With *grace?!*" I splutter, ready to tell him just how *graceful* I'll be when Hunter squeezes my hand, hard. "And what is my punishment?" I say instead.

Salam bares his teeth, his neon eyes cold. "You will soon find out."

7

Warrior angels spill into the room in a white and golden wave, their faces impassive. They block the exit to hem us between them and the Creators. Uziyah stands alone, sneering proudly. Devinon and Hunter share a glance.

"This is not good," Dev says.

"None of this is good." Hunter tugs on my hand until I look into his eyes, his expression grave. "You must fight them, Maia. No matter what."

Panic claws at my chest and renders me speechless.

I knew this was coming. Something bad. Of course I did. The Creators weren't going to drag us onto their ship, give us a harsh talking to, then let us go.

"We did what you wanted." My words burst out, high and harsh. "We learned from your punishment. We've cleaned up our planet and are reversing the environmental damage. We did what you wanted."

Salam sniffs. Air whistles through the slim nostrils of his beak. "Too little, too late. Your race's embittered acceptance does not negate your act of rebellion. You are their figurehead. The instigator. You will be punished."

Salam straightens his long neck to peer over our heads at the gathered warriors.

"What about our angels?" I say, hating the wheedling tone creeping in.

"*Your* angels?" Salam snaps his beak. "Your arrogance is insufferable, human. Your civilisation has much to learn about humility. Let your fate be the lesson they need."

Okay, do not like *that* at all.

"Are the others subdued?" Salam says to the warriors crowding the doorway.

A female bows her head, her white, shining hair slithering across her perfect cheekbone. "Yes, Creator. It worked as you expected."

"As we designed," Salam corrects with a cluck of his tongue.

The female bows deeper, and her wings brush the floor. "Of course. You are the Creator."

Man, these guys. They really are arseholes.

Salam returns his beaky head to our level. Well, Hunter and Devinon's level. The Creator's violet gaze flicks between them.

"You are defective but you can be salvaged."

"We do not want to be salvaged," Hunter says.

"Your wants are of no consequence. You are a weapon. We direct and you obey."

"You made them intelligent and self-aware," I say through my teeth. "You can't force them to be slaves."

"I see no issue. If you had crafted a tool—primitive, obviously—would you not want it to perform as devised? And if it did not, would you throw it away? Your species consumes without cease. Be content that we do not."

My jaw clenches. "Our tools don't have thoughts and feelings of their own."

"And neither should ours."

Icy fear trickles down my spine.

Salam and Tallai raise an arm parallel to their concave chests. They splay their long digits on a device at their wrists. Hunter and Dev drop to their knees. I yelp, jerking my hand free before Hunter crushes my fingers.

Uziyah barks a mean laugh. "Hunter always looks better on his knees."

Hunter growls, his fingers tensed against the floor. His wings arch huge and black from his shoulders. Dev groans behind him and clutches his head, a shiver rustling his sapphire feathers.

"What are you doing?" I gasp.

"Controlling them," Salam says dismissively. He bobs at Uziyah. "Proceed."

Uziyah strides to Hunter and Dev. The sweep of his wing shunts me from his path. I trip over my own feet and join my husband and his best man on their knees. Uziyah unclips two metal collars from his cloth belt. The bands circle their throats with a brutal, final snap. Hunter lunges for Uziyah and drags the angel to the floor in a tangle of feathers. His hands give Uziyah a collar of flesh. Cartilage crackles under the pressure.

The band on Hunter's neck starts to glow a sickly green. It forms bright lines and dots through the sheen of metal—an alien artefact come to life. Hunter's flashing eyes and bared teeth smooth to arrogant perfection, though his grip stays on Uziyah's throat.

"Release him, Hunter," Salam says.

Hunter's fingers loosen. He gains his feet, flicking his wings and settling them against his back. Not once does he look at me. His dark gaze remains on the Creators. Devinon stands beside him, his lively eyes blank and calm.

"How may I serve you?" Hunter says.

His robotic voice has dread unfurling in my gut. He was like this when the Creators ordered the retreat from Earth. In thrall to the circuits in his brain. Not himself until he fought it off.

"Hunter?" I whisper.

He ignores me. I repeat it louder, distress and bile rising with the volume of his name. Black and empty eyes meet mine. There's nothing familiar in his face. No love, no affection. An expression of perfect arrogance but not the mask he wears to protect himself when he's feeling uncertain.

There is no mask.

"What have you done?" I breathe past the pulse in my throat.

Salam steeples his fingers under his chin. "Simply enhanced the desired behaviours he should have expressed."

I crawl to Hunter since my legs are too wobbly to support me. My tentative fingers brush the tight, criss-crossing laces of his knee-high boot.

"Hunter. You know who I am. Look at me. Really *look* at me."

My voice cracks. Hunter raises his awful, emotionless gaze to Salam.

"Do you wish me to dust her?" he says.

Salam clicks his beak. "No. She has much to learn."

My heart continues to pump but each beat is jagged, a sliver of glass slicing deeper. I can't stop the tears on my cheeks or the sobs ripping from my chest. They're as sharp as my pulse.

"Hunter?"

He ignores me. I hug myself, the pain in my stomach like a blow. Drops of moisture dampen the filthy skirt of my wedding dress.

"So this is my punishment?" I say, scowling through a watery blur at Salam. "You steal the man I love from the life he wanted and make him a monster. Don't you have enough of those? Why couldn't you have left us alone? All he wanted was to be safe. To fit in."

"And now he does, where he belongs—with the rest of his race." Salam tilts his bulbous bird head, his expression pitying. "Did you really think you could keep him? He is not yours to possess. He is our property and will be until he dies."

"You cannot have him," I snarl. "I'll find a way to reverse whatever shit you've done."

A kiss worked the last time, like any fairy tale. This may be a sci-fi space nightmare but I'll give it a shot.

I climb to my feet with as much dignity as I can muster in my ruined dress. My knees rattle together. I scrub at my face, no doubt smearing snot across my cheek.

"I expected as such." Salam can't sneer with his rigid beak of a mouth but his brow cants above the slash of his eye. "Your civilisation is like the beasts you call puppies—they do not learn their mistake until you shove their faces in it. You will accept your punishment with grace and quiet suffering, and I will show you why." He snaps his knobbly digits. "Bring her."

Hard fingers manacle my bicep. I flinch, and yank my gaze up to meet dispassionate eyes. Hunter's wedding ring pinches my skin. He looms, all black wings and shadows.

"Hunter"—my voice quivers—"you're hurting me. You said you'd never hurt me."

A beat of silence. I search his face, desperate for a hint of something, *anything*, to show he's in there. A relaxing of his grip, a spark. Maybe he's pretending. Going along with the ruse until an opportunity for rescue presents itself.

The grip tightens, crushing muscle against bone.

My semi-indestructible warrior angel husband drags me from the room.

8

I can't count the levels of the spaceship. There are no lifts or stairs, only curls of passageways taller than they are wide, with doorways accessed from the air. The Protectorate walk the turquoise path or fly above, zooming through the corridors in blasts of wind that stir my hair and chill the tracks of my tears. No other Creators cross our route, just Salam and Tallai marching in front while Hunter drags me behind, my arm throbbing and tingly under his grip. My pulse slams in my fingertips. Devinon and Uziyah stalk at the rear, striding abreast like old pals. Dev's face is blank. His eyes, when they deign to pass over me, hold no recognition or concern.

I hustle to match Hunter's long stride, though it doesn't ease his clamp on my bicep. I twist my body to stroke his knuckles, and trail higher to his muscled forearm through the rips in his shirt.

"Look at me, Hunter. *Please.*" The word breaks. "You have to fight this. Fight them. I can't do it without you. Please."

Hot fingers brand my wrist. Dark eyes meet mine.

"Do not touch me," he growls.

He releases my bicep and the muscle weeps in relief. Pins and needles bite along my skin. One hand traps both my wrists, his arm locked to hold me behind him and away from his body.

He yanks me onward like a prisoner on a rope. I stumble, nearly twisting my ankles in my heeled shoes.

No doubt he'd drag me on my face if I were to trip. He's a warrior angel. Cold and unfeeling. He's not my Hunter anymore.

More sobs try to bubble to the surface but I swallow them. They hurt all the way down.

After interminable minutes of stomping, we halt in a dead-end corridor. A headache zips between my temples at the constant brightness of the walls. Salam splays his freaky double-thumbed and multi-jointed hand on a slightly darker square of wall. A door clunks then hisses open, the outline of it indiscernible when it was closed.

Rustling comes from inside, and a yell of, "Fuck me, it's *Jurassic Park*."

A smile twitches at my mouth despite the burning in my wrists from the unfeeling weapon that used to be my husband. *Will be* my husband again.

"Steph!" I call over the gawky figures of Salam and Tallai.

"Maia! Are you all right?"

"Define 'all right'," I say, my voice wobbly.

We pile into a room similar to our bare cell on the shuttle, without all the swirling and reflections. A window looks onto the vastness of stars.

"Oh, Maia—your dress!" Steph laments.

Steph and Greg clutch each other in the centre of the room. More for her benefit than his, given the lines of strain carved into her face.

The stress won't be good for her condition. She's liable to get a flare up, and they can be brutal. How will she manage without her cane, her wheelchair, her meds? Or her angel who carries her around like she's a precious gem.

I glance at my wedding dress. Dried blood and dirt smudge the white silk. Steph and Greg's outfits fair no better. Steph's remaining shoe has been kicked off in the corner, her feet bare and vulnerable through the spill of her dress. Greg's suit jacket smothers her shoulders.

A frown wrinkles her brow. "What's going on?"

"Dev?" Greg glances at the collar on the angel's throat. "You okay, man?"

"Devinon," Salam says, "hurt the female."

"No!"

I wrench against Hunter's grip, bruising my wrists but tearing free from his hold. I manage one step then his fingers clamp my bicep on top of the red marks he's already left. He jerks me to a stop. I fight to pry his fingers off, wriggling like a fox in a trap. Hunter doesn't even look at me. His dark eyes follow Dev as he slips around the Creators and crosses the room.

"Blue-bear?" Steph says, hesitant. She searches his face.

"He's not himself." I hiss at the throbbing in my abused arm. "The collars are messing with their heads."

Dev grabs for Steph. Greg spins and shields her body with his. He slaps a palm to Devinon's chest, and shoves. Dev stands unmoved yet Greg gets shunted back, nearly tripping over Steph. Dev fists his hand in Greg's shirt and tosses him to the side, buttons flying. Greg screeches along the ground but scrambles to his feet and launches at Devinon before his fingers can close on the wide-eyed Steph.

"Blue-bear?" she says, a tear trailing down her cheek.

Greg wraps himself around Dev's side, arms and legs and all, but the angel peels him off. His hand grips Greg's throat and slams him into the window. Fingers tighten. Greg's heels kick at the wall.

"Dev," he chokes, clawing at the hand, "wake up, you stupid blue cunt."

"Let him go!"

Steph tugs at the arm throttling Greg. Devinon backhands her and sends her sprawling. She stares at him from a tangle of midnight-blue dress and long legs, blood on her mouth and heartbreak in her eyes. Greg's lips turn cyanotic.

"Stop it!" I yell, my arm numb from my struggles. "Whatever fucking lesson this is, I've learned it. I'll do what you want."

Salam nods at Dev. Dev removes his hand from Greg's neck and spins on his heel, not even watching Greg slide down the wall to crumple on the floor. Steph crawls to Greg, crying softly. She cuddles him against her chest while he hacks and wheezes, his brown hair in a frizzy cloud around his face.

"You will accept your punishment without any human scheming?" Salam says.

"Fine. Just leave them alone."

Salam bobs his bony head. "They will remain untouched, but heed this—for every act of defiance, I will send Devinon to them. He will bruise and break their flesh, and their pain will be on your conscience. Should you complete your punishment to my satisfaction, they will be returned to their savage home world unharmed."

"You'll let them go? Alive? As long as I, what—don't interfere with what you've done to Hunter?"

Salam makes an awful crunching, crackling sound deep in his long throat.

Christ, is that how a Creator laughs?

"That is only part of your punishment, human. I expect

much more from you."

"Can you understand what that big vulture is saying?" Steph whispers, her voice thick with tears.

It drags my attention from the gloating Creator. She sniffs hard, still cuddling Greg. He's a normal colour now, though his eyes are pink and watering. His breaths whistle in his throat. The marks of Dev's fingers bloom a deep red.

"They squirted something in my ears. It lets me understand their language."

"Cool," Greg croaks, attempting a quavering smile. "Nanotech?"

"This is not the time, idiot," Steph says affectionately, hugging him closer. Her gaze flicks to the silent and deadly Hunter attached to my arm. "What are they going to do?"

"They haven't been real descriptive on that part. Whatever else it is, they want me to be contrite and learn my lesson."

"These creatures and their fucking lessons," she hisses. "You attacked *us*, arseholes."

"Your companion would do well to hold her tongue," Salam says, scowling beneath the ridge of his crest.

I raise my chin and stare into his bright eyes. "You've made your point—you have my friends hostage and at your mercy. Just don't expect *them* to be graceful about it. Expecting it from me is enough."

Salam sniffs and stalks from the room, Tallai trailing in his wake. Hunter, Devinon and the strangely silent Uziyah herd me out the doorway.

"Be careful, Maia!" Steph says.

The muscled warriors block my view of her and Greg no matter how much I duck and twist. Hunter tugs me away. The door glides shut. More tramping along corridors as my arm goes dead. Salam pauses at an archway lined by some kind of frond. There's a noise beyond, like the sighing of wind through trees.

"I believe you wanted to issue the first challenge, Uziyah?" Salam says.

Uziyah grins, and his bared teeth shine in the light. "I challenge Hunter. It has been too long since he knelt for me."

Hunter offers no reaction except a slow, cool appraisal of the other warrior.

Salam clicks his beak. "Then let the fights begin."

9

The Protectorate spaceship contains a massive arena spanning multiple levels, if not every level.

Of course it does. Where else would they maul each other in their dominance fights?

Hunter and Uziyah leap over the balcony of our empty spectator box, accessed from the archway, and drop from view. Their wake stirs purple ferns that creep along the darkly transparent gallery. I wrap my shaking hands around the ornate pole peeking through the vegetation. Rough fronds catch at my skin and smell like rich earth and fungus. Salam and Tallai loom behind me.

The roof is a black rectangle onto more stars. Each level ends in a balcony covered in the same purple ferns. Warrior angels crowd the boxes opposite us, peering into the depths of the arena in perfect silence except for the rustle of wings. I balance on tip-toes to join them since the balcony is almost at chest height.

The floor of the arena is a shimmering gold not unlike the wings of the Creators' favoured angels. Hunter and Uziyah face off across the expanse five levels below. Both angels grip a glowing sword. Hunter twirls his, fast and expert, slicing the air with streaks of blue.

The movement reminds me of being cornered in the servants' corridors of Newhailes estate house. The icy waft of the eerie blue blade, and Hunter's perfect arrogance. My clumsy swordplay as I desperately parried his thrusts.

Hunter was hiding who he was—conforming as best he could yet never fitting in. But he's not pretending now. The collar has made him exactly what the Creators wanted—a weapon as hard and unfeeling as the blade in his hand.

The bruises on my bicep throb in synchrony to my heartbeat, each one in the shape of Hunter's fingers. Even the skin around my wrists is reddened from his grip. My hands look pale and vulnerable amidst the ferns.

"I hope you are ready to kneel, Hunter," Uziyah taunts, his sword slashing the air in front of him.

Hunter cocks his head. "Remember when I knelt, for it was the last time. Now, you will kneel for *me*."

Without any kind of signal, the angels launch at each other. Their swords clang, and the sound echoes to the roof. My fingers clench on the balcony. I lean out further, the pole a freezing brand across my chest. The hush of the arena raises goosebumps on my bare arms. That, and the hungry intensity of the spectating warriors.

Uziyah batters at Hunter, using his bulk to overwhelm. Except Hunter blocks and sidesteps easily, dragging his blade across Uziyah's broad chest for the first cut.

It would be first blood if angels actually bled for anything but iron.

A pale mouth opens in Uziyah's flesh. Uziyah hisses, propelling upwards to dodge the corresponding strike to his back. Hunter jumps, and the space fills with the beating of their wings, black against gold. They chase each other through the entire arena—swooping, slashing, twisting.

Their movements are too fast for me to follow. Streaks of blue and the smack of flesh on flesh. A grunt when metal parts skin. The rip of expensive silk not designed for warfare. Hunter is nothing but a black blur and a flashing sword.

Who the hell is winning?

The angels pause at the apex of the roof, their ribs heaving, wings flapping hard. More bloodless wounds yawn in Uziyah's flesh—pecs, arms, stomach. A rent in his loose trousers gives a glimpse of bulging thigh. He stares at Hunter with a flicker of panic in his eyes. His rival is unmarked, though his shirt is torn at the biceps and missing enough buttons to leave it gaping to his breastbone.

"Did you think this would be easy?" Hunter smirks, and twirls his sword. "The warrior you fought before was not me. Submit and spare yourself the pain of my blade." The smirk turns malevolent. "Though there will be other pain."

Uziyah manages a sneer, weak compared to the ones he tossed at us feeble humans. "This fight is not over yet. Not until you are broken."

I have to admire his bravado despite the greenish cast to his skin. The awful draw of the soulreaver is enough to sicken him even if it can't dust him. I thought I'd feel some petty satisfaction at seeing his defeat but dread churns in my stomach. And pity. I know, and Uziyah knows, what will happen to him when he loses.

The winner gets to take what they want.

"One of us will break," Hunter says, "but it will not be me."

Does Uziyah regret his mockery now? A smart warrior would have waited to see the effect of the collar before issuing a challenge. Because Hunter is right—he's not the angel he was. He's not anything I recognise. Is he still in there, aware but not in control? Slave to the beast in charge of his body?

He dives for Uziyah. Blades clash and ring. The warriors grapple and fall, wrenching free to hack and kick, their wings shivering furiously. Uziyah's thrusts are frantic and graceless. His sword wobbles beneath Hunter's unrelenting power.

Been there, done that. Did not enjoy.

Metal shrieks. A blade plummets point-down into the floor, the handle quivering. Small objects scatter and bounce around it. Uziyah's cry yanks my eyes to him. He cradles his arm to his chest, his hand absent at least three fingers. Hunter observes for a beat, his face empty, then rams his sword in Uziyah's gut. I wince at Uziyah's groan. Hunter draws the weapon free and spears Uziyah's wing in a puff of golden feathers. Uziyah falls, his ungainly flapping doing little to slow his descent. He thuds onto his feet but his legs crumple and spill him onto his face. Hunter stoops then spreads his black wings wide, landing gently. He kicks Uziyah onto his back and sets his blade to his throat.

"Submit," he says, the word toneless yet more terrifying than a growl.

Uziyah blinks, swallows. I almost miss his whispered, "I submit."

My nape prickles at the stirring of the spectating angels.

"Then get on your knees." Hunter lobs his sword to the side.

I back away from the balcony. Or try to. A pair of hunched and bony figures herd me forward, pressing me into the ferns.

"Witness the spoils of battle," Salam says, his beak grazing my scalp. "Hunter has finally reached his potential without the stain of your humanity."

I grit my teeth and refuse to look down. "Hunter never

wanted to be like this. It had nothing to do with my humanity."

"You enabled his weakness when we would have stamped it out." Cold fingers dig into my skull and tilt my head. "Now look, or I will take this as defiance."

I steel myself, and look.

Uziyah sways, hunched around his damaged hand and skewered gut. One golden wing is tucked to his back, the other flopped out, feathers ragged. Hunter tugs at the laces of his trousers.

Oh, god, I don't want to watch.

"*Witness,*" Salam hisses.

Tallai leans closer, swamping me, his tiny pupils fixed on the scene below. He smells like the newspaper at the bottom of a lizard tank. Salam tightens his grip on my head. Fingernails scrape across my hair.

Hunter holds his massive length in his fist. Uziyah, broken and sick on his knees, raises his gaze to Hunter's face. Whatever he sees makes his cheeks as ashen as his eyes.

"Hunter... wait—"

Hunter grabs a chunk of Uziyah's sunflower-yellow locks and forces his dick into Uziyah's mouth, not pausing until Uziyah gags and shoves at Hunter's hip with his uninjured hand. Hunter holds him in place, buried to the hilt, suffocating him. Uziyah's struggles weaken, his body going limp. Hunter pulls out. Uziyah manages half a gasp before he's choking again. Hunter pounds himself into Uziyah's face. The crack of Uziyah's jaw dislocating seems to echo through the arena but his screams are muffled.

Hunter doesn't stop.

I shut my streaming eyes. Bile scalds the back of my throat.

"How can you let them do this to each other?" I wheeze.

"This is *cruel*. And I don't even like Uziyah."

"Uziyah will heal. He will be motivated to fight better."

I shake my head, Salam releasing his grip while I struggle to ignore the slap of skin, the throttled shrieks.

"No matter how good you fight, someone always has to lose."

Salam snaps his beak. "Then make sure it is not you."

Hunter grunts, and the awful sounds cease. He steps back, tucking his slick, softening cock into his trousers and retying the laces. Uziyah slumps onto his one good arm, sheltered by the spill of his hair. His whole body shakes. Hunter crouches next to him and whispers something in his ear. The shaking quivers to his feathers.

Hunter straightens and tilts his face, his dark gaze finding me. Fear gathers in my throat.

Salam lifts a knobbly hand. "Take Uziyah to the healing ward where he can ruminate on his defeat. Hunter—stay. We have another challenge for you."

I swallow a groan.

I can't watch him mangle another angel. With his stamina, he could rape several more before he gets tired. If I have to 'witness' then I'm going to vomit all over the Creators. And the twisted arseholes will deserve it.

Two angels swoop to Uziyah and drag him upright, ignoring his whimpered protests at their rough handling. They fly through a spectator box, the warriors inside parting for them, and disappear into a corridor.

I wrench my gaze from Hunter, who's still staring up at us, waiting for his orders. His next challenger.

I feel sorry for the poor bastard, whoever they are.

"Can I not watch this one?" I say, then add a sincere, "Please?"

Salam and Tallai regard each other over my head, and their

eyes glow violet. Salam steps away, giving me a bit of space. He tips his crest at me.

"You do not have to witness."

I release a breath but it becomes a gulp when Tallai's chill fingers wrap around my bruised and aching bicep.

"You do not have to witness," Salam says again, his pointed teeth gleaming, "because now it is your turn."

10

There's no escape from the bottom of the arena. A smooth wall circles to the level of the first balcony where numerous faces peer down at me, bloodlust shining in their eyes. More bruises stipple my biceps from Tallai's tight hold. I kick and wriggle and make them worse. His wings stir his musty, reptilian scent until it catches in my throat. He deposits me on the floor and returns to the spectator box before I can grab his spindly, backward-jointed leg. My heels sink into the spongy surface. The gold material is pitted and stained from years of battle. Uziyah's sword remains embedded in the centre like Excalibur, separating me and Hunter.

He hasn't acknowledged me yet. His focus is on his Creators, his expression impossible to read.

"This is my challenge?" he says. "This feeble creature?"

I flinch. The musical underlay of the angel's language fails to soften the insult.

Salam leans over the balcony, aloof and imperious. "The challenge is hers. She alone may use a sword."

The blade glows blue and nauseating. Hunter's gaze drills into mine. He clenches his fists, tensing the muscles in his forearms. Dark wings arch from his shoulders.

The feathers are soft. Silken when they brush my skin. He

likes getting them sticky.

My heart lodges in my throat and pounds in my ears.

"Kill her," Salam says.

"What?" I gasp.

Hunter claims a step. I scuttle backwards.

"*This* is my punishment?" I screech. "Getting the man I love to murder me has nothing to do with your grace or learning my lesson bullshit."

Why am I surprised? The Creators are cruel. More savage than the worlds they judge. I encouraged a rebellion and sullied their unstoppable army. Tamed a warrior angel into a loving, gentle partner. What better sentence than to die at his hands?

Hunter cocks his head. "I am not a man."

A sob rips from my chest.

"You can't do this," I whisper. "You can't..."

"Cut him enough times with the blade and he will be too sick to fight," Salam says.

I shake my head, retreating further from the sword. "I can't hurt him. I won't. I love him."

"That is your weakness," Salam hisses. "A weakness you forced on our warriors. For that, you will suffer and regret." He points a finger at me and barks out a harsh and final, "Begin."

My back hits the wall of the arena, the surface cold on my bared shoulder blades. Hunter stalks towards me, predatory and unstoppable. Black hair falls into eyes that are no different to the spectating angels above. Hungry for blood and violence.

"Hunter... wait..." I falter, realising I sound like Uziyah. "Look at what I'm wearing. *Look*, Hunter. Please."

I slide around the wall, smoothing my hands on the silk over my ribs and hips, plucking at the material so it swirls around my feet. Hunter's expression doesn't change for the millisecond it drops to my outfit.

I lick my lips, my pulse difficult to speak past. "I'm in my wedding dress. It's our wedding day."

That's technically a lie. It's been six months for everyone on Earth. For me, it still feels like today. Today he told me he would love and protect me. Today he became my husband. Is it even day? There's no sunrise or sunset in space, only the steady burn of stars.

"These words mean nothing to me," Hunter says.

"You're wearing my ring on your finger. You promised to be mine, forever and always."

He knew this was coming. Something that would take him from me. He told me to fight, no matter what.

But how am I supposed to fight *him?*

He glances at his hand, thumbing the black band on his ring finger. I take advantage of his distraction and scramble for the sword. My dress tangles around my calves. The weapon's handle slides from my sweaty grip. I tug it free on the second try and hold it in front of me, the blade bobbing at Hunter. The thing is heavy. Hunter watches my movements, apparently unconcerned.

The sword won't kill him, not like the iron one I stabbed him with during our first fight in the servants' corridor of Newhailes. I'm hoping it will be a deterrent. The thought of sliding it into his flesh makes my stomach heave.

I open my mouth.

"She cannot submit," Salam says over me.

The bastard.

Hunter prowls low and wary, determination hardening his face. The weight of thousands of eyes settles on my shoulders. My blade twitches. The chill wafting from it chases goosebumps up my quivering arms.

If I nick myself with it, I'll crumble to dust.

"You don't have to do what they say." I retreat carefully in my heels, my gaze locked on Hunter. "You're better than them."

"They are my creators. I am their weapon."

"You're more than a weapon."

Hunter bares his teeth. "No, I am not."

My spine hits the wall at the same moment he lunges for me. I yelp, swiping with the sword to keep him at bay. He ducks under the whistling blade and grabs my wrist, ripping the weapon from my fingers. It sails across the arena and clangs into a wall. He shifts his hold, both hands wrapped around my forearm and lifting it between us. The collar circles his throat and casts a sickly glow on the flesh beneath. His hands tighten.

I touch his knuckles, my fingers trembling. "I love you, Hunter. I know you can fight this. I trust you."

His black eyes show my pale reflection but nothing else.

Bones snap under his palms.

My scream echoes to the roof of the universe.

Blinded by tears, I stumble away, unsure if Hunter released me or if I thrashed myself free. My arm is a supernova of agony, jolting every time I move and sending stabs of pain through my body. My heel tangles in the hem of my dress, and I slam onto my uninjured side. The impact scrapes my shattered bones together. I blink or pass out. Strong fingers grip my leg, bending it, my dress parting to my thigh. I roll onto my back to stare up at my husband.

"No, Hunter." His name cracks as easily as my bones. "Don't hurt me. Don't let them win. I love—"

He breaks my calf over his knee as if it were kindling. My leg flops at a grotesque angle. Vomit floods my mouth and turns my howl bubbling and broken. I drag myself through the acid stench of my own stomach contents. Shock narrows my vision to a fizz of white.

A prod of a boot returns me to my back. Bile stains the bodice of my dress and clumps in the corners of my mouth. It tastes of rotten lemons and despair.

"Hunter."

I don't recognise my voice—reedy and lost. Scratchy from screaming. I impeach him with my hand, palm outward. The gems on my wedding ring glint in the light. The pain of my tortured limbs mutes to a throb.

Warm fingers circle my wrist. I'm crying, repeating his name over and over. He braces a foot on my shoulder, and tugs. My joint pops from the socket. My shriek sounds like the rage of a dying animal. The arena goes a bit hazy.

A figure looms over me—the angel of death. Nothing but shadows. A whisper of wings as he crouches.

Those same warm fingers wrap around my throat and cut off my air. My mouth gapes. I can't even claw at him. I kick weakly but he's on the side of my shattered leg. Delicate cartilage crackles under his grip. The need to breathe fills my lungs with fire. My spine arches and sends those flames to the fractured ends of my bones.

I stare at Hunter, beseeching him. My eyes feel swollen. All my blood is trapped in my head and pounds along to my frantic pulse. Pain sizzles between my temples.

I pray for him to see me, *know me*. Remember. His body is there. The body I've loved and explored. The hands crushing my throat are the same hands that have stroked and held and driven me to ecstasy. The lips have kissed and teased and whispered, "I love."

How can it end like this?

Hunter leans closer. His wings flare in triumph. Something snaps under his hands. Something important. Numbness sweeps through me and swamps my vision in darkness. A ringing in my ears rises to a crescendo.

I die, broken in the hands of a warrior angel.

One that's no longer mine.

11

The afterlife is a warm, humming blanket wrapped around me from neck to toes. I drift in the quiet, replaying memories since they're all I have left—Hunter, prickly and distrustful when I decided to help him and nurse him back to health. His silent intensity and wary inquisitiveness. The way he'd cock his head and say, "What is…?" for any word he didn't understand. How he held me on our first flight together. His protectiveness. My increasing attraction for the lonely, stubborn angel who just wanted to be gentle.

What hope is there for him now? What kind of life? He's the weapon the Creators wanted—sharp, violent and unquestioning. His existence will become one long battle between dominating his brethren and punishing wayward civilisations. He'll service his creators when they demand it because who doesn't want to shag their own tools? They built it, therefore they can stick whatever they want in it. Or have the tool stick it to them…

I don't know. It's hard to follow my thoughts in this floaty place.

Is Hunter aware? *My* Hunter. What if he's trapped in his body, but sentient? A passenger forced to watch. The thought of his suffering makes me want to scream and smash things. I don't want him to have witnessed what he did to me when he broke me into pieces, unable to intervene. Unable to stop it. He would have tried. Raged and railed against his flesh and bone prison. At least, for both our sakes, he'd killed me instead of claiming his victory. Like he'd claimed Uziyah. Silver lining to being dead, I guess. He'll never have to watch himself rape me. I'd rather he was asleep in there. Cushioned and safe, like I am wherever this is.

I wish I could have saved him. But what am I supposed to do? I can't fight death. I would if I could. For Hunter. I'd punch that cowl-wearing, scythe-carrying arsehole right in the face.

Maybe Hunter will eventually struggle free of the collar's influence. When he discovers what the Creators made him do, none of them will escape his wrath.

They better have sent Steph and Greg home now that I'm dead. Will my friends know what it means? Will they resist, desperate to rescue Devinon and Hunter themselves? Demand to see my broken corpse as proof? Steph won't go quietly. Greg will convince her. He's had a crush on her since our apocalypse. He won't let anything happen to her.

I always wanted them to form their own triad—Steph, Greg and Dev—though I have no idea if Greg swings that way. Steph finally has the body she was meant for but Dev is all male. I got the impression the angel would be open to it. He likes to tease Greg, and watch him. But maybe Steph only considers Greg a friend.

Is it weird to want your best friends to be in a polyamorous relationship? It's not that I'm thinking of them in a threesome or anything. I don't picture them having sex. I just want them to be happy.

Not that it matters. Dev is as trapped as Hunter. He'd kill Steph and Greg if the Creators willed it.

Have they got rid of my body already? I'm not sure how much time has passed. Did they cremate me or give me a space burial? Maybe my drifting corpse will find its way into the Oort Cloud with all the other junk.

Again, I don't know. My thoughts are ephemeral and disjointed. I should rest. I can't shut my eyes since they're already shut. I think. Do I even have eyes? I'm so tired. Uncomfortable as well, which seems unfair. My bones ache. Why am I even feeling my bones? Maybe it's like a phantom limb, except all of me is the phantom. Yet the warm fuzziness is slipping away as my mind clamours louder. Insistent. Telling me something. Telling me to—

"Wake up now, child."

The soft, calming words whisper over the vibration of buzzes and clicks.

My eyelids flutter.

I have eyelids. That means I have a body. I guess that's good. The afterlife would be kind of boring if I was just an amorphous ball of gas that thought too much.

"Keep following my voice."

Crap. Is she God? I believed in her once but I'll have to apologise for my loss of faith. I'm sure she'll forgive me.

I squint against a silver light that halos my vision in rainbows. Blinking resolves the brightness into a mirrored ceiling like the one in the domed room where they collared Hunter and Dev. I try to move but my arms and legs are pinned, constricted by the blanket, which continues to hum. A weight settles on my shoulder. Squeezes.

"Do not struggle, child. The healing cycle is almost complete."

"What?" I croak.

A tube prods between my lips. I suck, and the familiar tang of the drink we had in the shuttle soothes my throat. My eyes water from the tartness. A shadow leans over me. My heart skips at the black wings but they're scaled, not feathered, with diamonds of powder blue and pink.

Bronwyn'challi. The healer.

Bloody hell, I'm not dead.

The swaddling around me beeps and hisses, relaxing suddenly. Bronwyn gathers it in her long arms then feeds it into a glass orb in the centre of the hexagonal room, my bed along one edge of the wall. Mist fills the globe at the press of a button. A tank containing pink liquid sits next to the orb and reminds me of the goo in the stasis pods. The surface ripples. Opposite me, Uziyah lies on a cushioned slab, eyes closed, his arms crossed over his massive chest. His jaw looks normal, though the rest of his wounds are covered by some kind of clear gel.

"He will heal on his own," Bronwyn says, tracking the direction of my gaze. "To use the shroud would be a waste of resource."

"So why have it on a spaceship full of them?"

I turn my head as Bronwyn swishes to my side, her winged and angular frame blocking my view of Uziyah. The roof above me slopes to the reflective peak, the silver glow bathing the room.

"For creatures such as you, who need healing during punishment. And for ourselves, though we are not often injured during our duties."

I sit up carefully, flinching at Bronwyn's assisting hands

despite her gentle touch. I stroke my forearm, a slight ache in the bone the only sign it was broken. The same throb flares in my shoulder and my shin. My fingers shake when they touch my neck. It hurts when I swallow.

"Where is Hunter?" I say.

"I do not know, child."

"How long have I been here?"

"Not long."

A tight, mauve bodysuit hugs my slim frame, bunching around my ankles and wrists but otherwise fitting perfectly. Moulded to where I'm clearly not wearing a bra.

I may not have much in the boob department but I still have nipples, and the air is cool now I'm no longer swaddled in the 'shroud'.

I hug my chest. "Did I die?"

Bronwyn clicks her tongue. "We may be advanced, child, but even we cannot reanimate the deceased. As long as your brainwaves have not deteriorated, our healing devices can revive you."

"So why would Salam order Hunter to kill me?"

Air whistles in Bronwyn's nostrils. "Salam'ack'tai'moran is conducting your punishment. He will decide what means are fitting."

"*Fitting?*" I screech. "You're sick, you know that?"

"I am not unwell."

"Sick in the head," I say through my teeth. "It is not *fitting* or justified to turn my husband into an unthinking weapon you use to hurt me."

Bronwyn spreads her hands then tucks them under her chin. "We act for the greater good. If one creature's fate can sway the minds of others from committing crimes against nature and the universes then that lesson is a valuable one."

"Why don't you help the other civilisations, share your knowledge, instead of punishing them?"

"Because pain is heeded far better than pleasure, child."

"You punished us already." I swipe a tear from my cheek. "You didn't have to take him from me, too."

Pity softens Bronwyn's amethyst and navy eyes. "He was not yours to keep."

"He was mine. He *is* mine. He decided for himself the second he escaped your cruelty. He's not a tool or a machine. He's *mine*."

Silent tears drip from my jaw. Bronwyn dips her head but meets my glare.

I've still never seen one of the scaly bastards blink.

"It is better to accept your fate than rebel against it. You will only hurt yourself."

"No, *you're* hurting me. You're choosing to hurt me because my world fought back, and won."

"Yes, child, and the others must learn why such a path is foolish. It is the only way to achieve peace. Once your world abandons its savagery, you will be accepted into our empire and you will thank us for our stern guidance. We bring order from chaos, we do not thrive in it."

I rub my forehead. "And how exactly do you spread these 'lessons' to the other worlds? You didn't try to sway us. You just sicced your angels on Earth with zero contact before that."

"We did not… We will have…" Bronwyn clears her throat. "We would have spoken to your leaders. Perhaps our message was not taken with the gravity in which it was meant."

"Or there was no message."

"There are only so many worlds we can reach. Your

punishment here will teach others."

"How? You video my torture and send it to another civilisation? Tell them—submit, or else?"

"We"—a swift ruffle of wings—"do not record what happens here for others. Our word is our truth. That is enough."

"So what you say, goes?"

Bronwyn cocks her head. "Our word is truth."

"So Salam says Hunter is nothing but a weapon, which means it's true? Even though Hunter is a sentient being with wants and feelings of his own?"

"It was not his purpose to want."

"But he does," I say softly. "He did."

"He should not."

I sigh, and it seems to come from my toes. "I'm too tired to argue. You abuse everyone, even your own creations, and say it's for the greater good. But it's not."

I scrub my eyes. Bronwyn settles her wings, watching me in silence. She shifts her attention to her painted toenails.

"I must alert Salam'ack'tai'moran and Tallai'sig'chai that you are awake. Do not try to leave or you will be stopped by the field calibration of the door."

She stalks from the room. I give up trying to puzzle out what she meant. Where am I going to go anyway? I have no idea where I am in the spaceship, no idea where Steph or Greg's cell is, no idea where to find Hunter.

The loneliness threatens to crush my chest but I force myself off the padded slab instead of curling into a ball. My bare feet slap on the cold floor. I sidle over to the misty orb and pink tank, keeping them as barriers between me and Uziyah. A strand of sunflower-yellow hair sticks to his lips.

I need allies. Both of us have been beaten by Hunter. Maybe

we could work together, however reluctantly. I tamed an angel once, though he wasn't as much of a dick as this one.

"Uziyah?" I whisper.

No response. Damn. Hunter was immune to external stimuli when he was in a healing coma, except for one thing.

I creep forward. Uziyah's wing droops to the floor. Up close, the gold is a sheen over the white feathers. I pinch the edge of velvety flesh then scuttle behind my barricade. Uziyah snaps awake. Eyes the colour of dirty snow find me, narrowing to nothing but black, dilated pupil.

"Um, hi," I say. "Are you okay?"

He hisses. "What are you doing here, feeble creature?"

Funny, it doesn't hurt as much when he calls me it.

"I was Hunter's challenge after you."

Uziyah snorts. "You are not a challenge."

"I'm sorry for what he did to you. For what the Creators make you do. It doesn't have to be like this. We can help each other."

I'm still not great at the rousing speeches.

Uziyah's glare narrows further. "Help? *You* are the reason I am here. Hunter was weak. Easily dominated. Now he has been recreated to a better version of himself. This is your fault. You stupid, meddling, pitiful human."

Uziyah swings his legs off the side of the slab. He grits his teeth, flinches, and curls his fists. Clear gel oozes between his fingers.

"You will pay for my defeat," he says.

I retreat to the door but dare not risk stepping through and finding out what Bronwyn meant by field calibration. Uziyah prowls towards me and we circle the room, the orb and tank the only things separating us.

He must be too injured to launch himself at me.

"Stop running," Uziyah growls. "You achieve nothing except to anger me further."

"You stop, and listen for once." I speed up, getting breathless and a little dizzy. "You can't possibly want this life. Never-ending battle and brutality. No intimacy or kindness or *rest*."

"Weaknesses," he spits.

"Uziyah," I pant, "please—"

A hand clamps on my shoulder, two thumbs digging in.

"I see you are recovered enough to stand, Uziyah," Salam says. "You may return to your quarters."

Something flickers over Uziyah's face—regret, fear?—before it's gone beneath a mask of arrogant obedience. He bows to Salam and Tallai, glowering at me until he passes through the doorway without any hindrance, his wings and posture stiff.

Maybe Bronwyn lied to keep me from leaving.

She fusses around the room, her back to the rest of us. Salam spins me, both the Creators crowding close. I crane my neck to meet their violet gazes and force myself not to tremble.

"I am glad to see you are recovered also," Salam says. "Now we may continue."

"Continue? What do you mean *continue?*"

Salam and Tallai make the awful choking, laughing sound in their throats.

"Did you think that was your punishment? One challenge in the arena?"

Salam and Tallai wrap a hand around each of my wrists. Still cackling, they tow me towards the door. I dig in my heels. My bare skin slides and squeaks on the smooth floor. Tallai waves the device on his bony wrist at a panel beside the entrance. Nothing seems to happen but they tug me through into another corridor of pearl and turquoise, and I don't get zapped or whatever it was supposed to do.

"Your punishment is not to die at the hands of your beloved *once*," Salam says. "Your punishment is to suffer and heal until you break."

He cocks his head, pinning me with one bright, pitiless eye.

"And Hunter is waiting."

12

The arena is silent and still, the rest of the Protectorate absent instead of watching me with expressions of disdain and hunger. Salam and Tallai peer down from their spectator box—two vultures waiting to pick over my carcass. Fear and relief clash at the sight of Hunter, unharmed. He stands at the other end of the oval space, his wings slightly spread, a sword in his grip. No blue, deadly glow along the blade.

I guess even their fancy healing shroud couldn't revive me from a pile of dust.

Hunter is still wearing his black, laced trousers and boots but his wedding shirt is gone, replaced with one of his long-sleeved tops that's loose at the neck to show a slab of chest. The cuffs flop over his slim-fingered hands. His hair falls into his black eyes and tickles his sharp cheekbones. He is darkness and marble and an endless, predatory patience.

I ache to rush across the spongy floor and wrap myself around him. Hug him tight and inhale his intoxicating scent of ice. I miss him so much it hurts my stomach. It doesn't matter that he's right there, as beautiful and intimidating as always. It's not him.

Will it ever be him?

I push the question away, ignoring the prickle in my eyes. I thought I was dead before, that he was lost forever. As long as he's alive and I'm alive, I won't stop fighting for him.

I promised to protect him, too.

The glint of the ring on his finger fills me with hope. He hasn't taken it off, though a warrior would, not wanting anything to obstruct his grip or interfere with his weapons. Is Hunter in there, struggling to return?

"Draw your sword or Hunter will attack and this challenge will be as short and pathetic as the last," Salam says from his lofty vantage point, sneering down his beak at me. "Though I predict it will be so, whether you are armed or not."

A panel slides open in the wall beside me to reveal a single sword in a rack. The blade is dull, grey and speckled with rust. The metal scrapes as I pull it clear. Flakes drift to my toes.

"This is iron," I gasp, my gaze zipping to the Creators.

"Yes, one of the few things that can destroy him. The vulnerability to an Earth metal was an anomaly we did not plan. This element is not present in our universe."

"So why give me the means to hurt him now when you got all pissy about us damaging your property before?" My brittle laugh cuts Salam off before he can respond. "Because you know I won't kill him."

Salam bobs his head. "That is your weakness, not his. As he will demonstrate."

"It's not a—"

My retort becomes a yelp as Hunter leaps for me, his wings flapping and stirring my hair into a tangled mess. His blade slices in a perfect arc. Metal rings when mine meets it, the impact thudding through my arms. The tips of his feathers brush my ribs and the soft caress, even in the middle of him trying to kill me again, sends a spear of longing in my chest.

He kicks out and I roll away from his lashing boot, bruising my shoulder on the floor. He lands, head cocked, his dark eyes assessing.

"Remember when they imprisoned you in the research lab? Our government—the Scottish Government." I retreat while Hunter stalks me, and we dance across the arena. "They wanted to contain and study you. I got a panicked phone call that first night after I cried myself to sleep. You kept breaking out and wrecking stuff, demanding to know where I was, and nothing they injected you with sedated you. Later, they found out gas worked for a little while, much to your disgust. But until then, they begged me to come and get you under control."

Hunter offers no reaction to my babbling description. No flicker of remembrance or interest. Like all angels, he fights in silence. He jumps, and thrusts for my chest. I parry and spin clear, my sword ringing and scattering rust.

"When I arrived at the lab, you were breaking their very expensive electron microscope into tiny pieces and telling them that resistance was futile." Fondness tightens my throat. "You scooped me in your arms and carried me off into a storage cupboard where they heard way more than they bargained for. But it calmed you down. They grudgingly let me visit every day after that until we managed to get you freed."

Hunter attacks, his movements strong and fluid. I shut my mouth to concentrate on blocking each strike. Clanging swords and my harsh breathing are the only sounds. Sweat trickles down my back. My bones throb, my muscles starting to quiver. Hunter bares his teeth as I put more space between us.

"You love sugar. It's like catnip to you. If you, uh, were a cat."

Hunter arrows through the air. I swipe his sword, and hop

clear. He flaps hard, spinning around, his hair flopping over his forehead. He clenches his weapon in both hands, the blade in front of his face. Gorgeous and terrifying.

"I took you to the supermarket. You found the doughnuts all lined up in a cabinet. You managed to eat a whole box by the time I got you to the cashier." I roll again, groaning when my recently healed shoulder slams into the floor. The strain shows in my voice. "Only the promise of sex stopped you scoffing the rest on the flight home. You pounced on me as soon as the door shut. It was sweet and sticky and amazing. But then, you like sticky. Right, Hunter?"

"What is—" He shakes his head, his jaw bulging.

I scuttle clear from a fury of blows.

He's too fast for me. His stamina far surpasses mine. And I'm flagging.

A sharp line of heat flares across my left bicep, parting bodysuit and skin. Blood seeps into the material and dribbles to my elbow.

"Stop talking," Hunter barks. "Resistance is futile."

"But you like it when I stand my ground," I say, trying not to wheeze. My heart attempts to hammer past my ribs.

He silences me with another whistling, shrieking barrage of blades. More biting wounds open on my arms, my stomach. A nasty one across my thigh.

I limp a couple of steps, and gulp air. Crimson stains my bodysuit and streaks my skin.

"You like—warm baths. Cuddles. And hot chocolate. You love—to watch—the sun rise and set. You fall asleep when I read to you."

"Finish this, Hunter," Salam says. "This pathetic display has gone on long enough. You are letting a human defy you. A *human."*

I spare a weary glare for Salam and Tallai, who are apparently bored because I'm not bleeding out quick enough. I almost miss Hunter's move. I catch his cleaving strike on my blade but the force judders through my body. I cry out, and blood flows faster. I barely keep up with his next series of blows, earning myself a slice on the shoulder.

"How are you trained in swordplay?" Hunter growls.

"You. You taught me. We've practised—twice a week—for the last year."

"Why would I teach you?"

"Because you love me."

"What is love?"

I stuff my fist in my mouth to trap a sob, tasting copper and salt. My eyes blur.

He asked me that question in Steph's flat in Martello Court, right on the cusp of our rebellion. Steph smirked as I fumbled through an explanation of intense emotional attachment and being unable to imagine your life without the other. Then Hunter flew me back to Newhailes and proved he understood completely. He made love, and told me he loved.

"It's what you feel for me," I say around my knuckles.

I try to catch my breath, grab some respite, but exhaustion drags at me. My vision flares black then white. The floor shifts under my feet.

"I feel nothing for you," Hunter says.

I shake my head then regret it as wooziness somersaults from my brain to my gut. My tears taste of blood.

"That's not true," I whisper. "That collar around your throat is suppressing who you are. Take it off. Take it off and see."

He brushes a fingertip over the sickly glow of the band.

Salam and Tallai flick their wings, their scales hissing their impatience. Or unease? Are they afraid he'll remove the collar? Could it be that easy?

"Take it off, Hunter," I say, stepping closer. My knees wobble. "Please, take it off."

His hand drops to the pommel of his sword.

"This is who I am," he says.

His blade catches me diagonally across the chest. Blood splatters the floor. I shriek at the sizzling pain and stagger backwards, clutching at the wound, my hands slippery and red. My sword bounces at my feet, nearly lopping off a toe.

Time slips away from me. A hard thud finds me on my arse, blinking up at Hunter. Blood warms my belly and pools in my lap. I struggle to focus on him. The shape of him—broad shoulders, broader wings, narrow hips and pure, lean muscle.

My teeth chatter. Shivers wrack my body, and my blood weeps faster.

"Take it off," I say, my tongue somehow swollen and slurring. "Take it off, unless you're afraid. Take it off—"

Cool metal kisses my neck. Hunter's black eyes are all I can see. Everything else is mist and shadows. His pupils have swallowed the midnight-blue.

"I am not afraid," he says.

The sword slashes sideways. Burning, tearing pain. My scream becomes a gargle. Bright flashes blind my eyes, and I can't tell if I'm sitting up, lying down or floating off into space.

I try to breathe, and drown in the copper of my own blood.

13

There's fluid in my lungs. Of course there is. Hunter slit my throat, no hint of hesitation.

Am I still in the arena, gargling on my own blood? Is he watching me die? I guess I should be grateful our fights don't end in Hunter claiming his victory the Protectorate way—by taking what he wants. Like what he did to Uziyah. The dying part isn't exactly fun but I'm not sure I could survive the brutality of his touch. To be raped by the body that no longer belongs to the angel I love.

Hunter the Creators' tool doesn't care that I'm a tiny, fragile human. He doesn't want to be gentle.

I sob but it's muffled. Warm liquid fills my mouth and swirls at the movement. Everything is pink and blurred.

Did I get blood in my eyes?

My arms twitch. My knuckles rap off a smooth, hard surface. I blink, and my lashes sweep through fluid. It surrounds me. Cushioning me, though my spine bounces against the bottom. The floor? I paddle my limbs. My skin squeaks against the walls. Smooth edge meets smooth edge to form a box. A *coffin*.

My pulse rushes in my ears. I hold my breath. Was I breathing before? The liquid tastes like cardamom and honey. Sweetness to drown in.

I claw at the lid. My back and skull hit the bottom when I shove but, even with the extra leverage, the top doesn't move. It bruises my knees. My chest burns and my heartbeat throbs in my eyeballs. I thrash against the confines, vaguely aware that I'm not making any bubbles.

Shouldn't the last of my air escape as bubbles?

My vision stutters black and pink. My struggles weaken. I inhale without meaning to, unable to fight my own body. Fluid quenches the fire in my chest and throat. The disconcerting flow of warmth curls to my gut and rolls like a playful cat.

The hard surface of the top disappears from under my palms. Cool air caresses my skin. I jackknife upright, breaking the surface of the liquid and splattering it everywhere. Pink stuff gushes from my mouth as I hack and wheeze and cough. My flailing hands strike something firm, and a puff of air tickles my wrist.

"Careful, child," Bronwyn says, though I can't see her from my streaming, shuttered eyes. "The regenerative liquid is expensive to replenish. You must not spill it."

I vomit cardamom and honey. Liquid crackles in my lungs with every breath. The healing ward finally sharpens into focus.

I'm sitting in the glass tank of pink goo in the centre of the room. Liquid drips down the sides and plops on the floor. Globs of the stuff speckle Bronwyn's bodysuit. She scrapes her fingers through it and shakes the gloop back into the tank, leaving no dampness or stain on her clothes. I pat my hair. Totally dry.

A hysterical laugh catches in my throat. My heart is beating too fast. I want to scream but I'm scared I won't stop.

I touch my neck. My fingers tremble so much, they keep

dipping into the hollow between my collarbones. The goo ripples around me.

"How?" I croak. I swallow and try again. "How am I not dizzy? Sick? I lost… a lot of blood."

The ghostly slash of Hunter's blade flares across my throat. I wrap my fingers around my intact flesh, my shoulders hunched. My pulse skitters under my thumb.

"The healing bath, child. It repairs injuries to the circulation. Internal wounds. It replaced what you lost. Come."

Bronwyn twitches her long fingers at me. She coaxes me to kneel then hoists me out of the bath, her firm grip on my waist. The liquid slides thickly down my legs, as if reluctant to let me go. The slashes in my bodysuit show my untouched skin, my blood leached from the material or gobbled by the bath. But I feel each slice, like an echo of memory.

Bronwyn bustles around. I stay by the tank, chilled and exhausted. My teeth chatter. Everything is hazy yet still too bright. Bronwyn appears in front of me, though I swear she was on the other side of the room a second ago. I startle, and her cool fingers on my elbow keep me from colliding with the tank.

Probably best I don't wreck it. No doubt I'll need it again.

The horrible urge to giggle clogs my throat. My ribs heave but I can't catch my breath.

"Drink," Bronwyn says.

Something brushes my temple almost tenderly, but by the time I look up, Bronwyn's hand is at her side. She holds a metal beaker out to me.

The shuttle drink. Is that all they have for sustenance on the spaceship? It's bloody boring.

The tartness clears the fog from my head. My fingers clench

around the cup, and I stare at the dregs.

"Can I stay here?" I whisper. "Just for a little longer."

Her wings rustle. "No, child."

She sounds almost sorry.

A drop of clear water plinks into the empty beaker. My next inhale is thick and choked.

"Please?"

"Is she ready?"

I jump at the harsh voice. The beaker slips from my hands and clangs on the floor. Uziyah sneers at me from the doorway but it's better than Salam and Tallai and the burning judgement of their gaze, even if he wanted to hurt me the last time we were alone together.

He needs to get in line.

Bronwyn pauses. "She is ready."

My gaze zips to her. She scoops the cup off the floor and turns her back, her wings scrunched tight.

Was that reluctance? Was she about to lie to Uziyah to let me stay longer? It could just as easily have been a dispassionate assessment of my condition, and my own wishful thinking.

I have no friends here.

My bare feet drag but I make it across the room to Uziyah without crumpling to my knees. His hair is tied in a long ponytail, the sword absent from his hip. His sooty eyes track the marks of the blade in the material of my bodysuit. The cut over my chest runs from the top of my right boob to my left shoulder. He meets my gaze yet his face reveals nothing.

"How's your jaw?" I say.

Something flickers but he narrows his eyes, and it's gone. He spins on his heel and marches into the corridor. I cast a last glance around the hushed atmosphere and relative safety of the healing ward. Bronwyn remains with her diamond-patterned wings to me. I swallow what might be a whimper, and trail after Uziyah.

"Hurry up, feeble creature," he barks.

"You can call me Maia, you know."

"I will call you nothing, because that is what you are."

I stumble in his wake, struggling to coordinate my limbs. Dread fills my bones with metal and glass.

"Where are you taking me? Not"—my voice cracks—"not the arena?"

"You are to be given to Hunter to do with as he wishes. He is in the sleeping quarters."

My hand on the wall steadies me. The material is as cold as the rest of the ship. Goosebumps prickle my arms.

"And what does Hunter wish?"

Uziyah tosses a sneer over his shoulder. "Like the rest of us, he wishes for you to die. But I hope he gives you to me first."

My breath hitches, stutters, stops. I can't make my legs move. I want to curl up in a ball and cry until the pain goes away. I want to be with Steph and Greg. I want a hug. I want—

"Why are your eyes always leaking?" Uziyah huffs. "You are so weak."

I glare at him through my tears. "You're punishing me for having the audacity to not lie down and die. For rescuing Hunter and the others from this savagery you call a life. You could have joined us. You could've had something *better*, but you're just a stupid puppet."

Warm fingers wrap around my newly knitted throat and squeeze in warning. My shoulders hit the wall. Feathers flick in anger, bringing the scent of brine and sand.

"I am not a puppet, I am a *weapon*," Uziyah snarls.

"I could've been your friend."

"I do not need a friend."

"Everybody needs friends, Uziyah," I say softly, my voice hollow. It takes all my energy to look at him. "Especially you. I know all about your culture. You'll be challenged more now. I bet you've made a few enemies in those you've dominated. Hunter will keep challenging you."

Uziyah's throat bobs but he bares his teeth. "Then I will fight, and win."

"Or spend all your time on your knees." I place my hand over Uziyah's where he grips my throat. "It sure sounds like that person could use a friend."

He rips his hand from mine. For a second, he almost cuddles it to his chest. He clenches it into a fist instead.

"You will walk and you will be silent," he says, "or… or I will ignore my orders and deliver you broken."

He stalks down the corridor. I shut my mouth and follow but my lips twitch into the hint of a smile.

I blank the horrible part about breaking me and focus on the threat to go against his orders. The hiccup in his response. He thought, even for a second, about ignoring the demands of his creators and doing what he wanted. Have I gotten under his skin? Rattled him into a hint of actual individuality? Okay, so we need to work on what he wants so it doesn't involve smashing me into bits, but still…

Maybe there's hope for him yet. Maybe there's hope for all of us.

14

The sleeping quarters is a massive square room spanning several levels, judging by the openings to multiple corridors reached only from the air. The space is full of the rustle of wings but no other sound—no laughter, no chatting before bed, no camaraderie. Just stony, stoic warriors and the whisper of feathers. Narrow pallets line the floor, thin enough to offer no cushioning against the hard surface. Other pallets hang in rows to the ceiling without any obvious means of suspension.

Do they just freaking *float?*

The shifting of bodies falls silent. Every face turns to the lower doorway where Uziyah and I have entered. Their hatred blasts towards me in a wall of suffocating heat. My feet refuse to move. Uziyah points to the centre of the room then gestures again with more impatience when I dither at the entrance. He stomps towards the far edge without a backwards glance. Hunter sits on his pallet, watching us both, his elbows resting on his knees. His black wings brush the narrow aisles on either side of his bed—though calling it a bed is generous.

He told me he was used to sleeping on the floor but this is ridiculous. Do they get no comfort at all? No luxury to ease their harsh existence?

"Uziyah," he says in his soft and menacing voice.

Uziyah, who was giving Hunter a wide berth, pauses a few rows down. He doesn't turn but tension sings across his hulking shoulders.

Hunter surges to his feet with the grace of a jaguar. "You will swap with me."

Uziyah's wings arch protectively before he straightens them with an arrogant flare. He spares Hunter a haughty glance.

"Or I can challenge you for it," Hunter says, his tone indicating he would enjoy that very much.

Uziyah sticks his chin in the air and stomps back to Hunter's pallet. Before Uziyah can dodge around him, Hunter grabs his jaw, his fingers blanching Uziyah's flesh.

"You are mine now. Whenever I want."

Uziyah bares his teeth. "You defeated me once. I will not be surprised again."

"We shall see," Hunter says, his smile cruel.

He shoves Uziyah's head away, forcing the other angel to stagger a step. He sweeps past him and settles on a pallet at the edge of the room, his back to the wall. A better position than the centre, where he was surrounded on all sides. Uziyah flops onto Hunter's vacated mat, facing away from him, his muscles tight.

I creep into the sleeping quarters. The malevolent attention of hundreds of angels prickles across my nape and sends goosebumps rushing under my tattered bodysuit. Their animosity weighs my steps and sets my fight or flight response to *fucking run*.

But they would chase. It's what they're built for. What Hunter is built for.

Is this the part where he rapes me? He's technically won twice now. He can do with me as he wishes. And the dominant always take.

"You should share the human," a voice from above says, freezing me in the middle of the room. "Let us have her. She is no challenge."

A male peers over a floating pallet at me. Brunette hair forms a halo around his head and curls past his cheeks. His brown eyes have the lazy intensity of a lion wanting to play with its food.

"Or give her to us to punish," says the female with the white, shining hair and perfect cheekbones who bowed so deeply to Salam in the domed chamber. She sneers at me from higher up. "The human has much to answer for. I would not believe this weakling was the one to discover a vulnerability and lead a rebellion unless I had seen it for myself. Let me carve her crimes into her flesh."

"The human is mine," Hunter says.

Warmth sparks behind my ribs. Hope. The possessiveness has to be a good sign, right? If he were as evil and uncaring as the Creators want him to be, he would throw me to his brethren without thought. He'd watch them tear me apart and enjoy the spectacle.

I scuttle over to him while trying not to look like I'm scuttling.

Prey scuttle. Frightened little mice. Not the leader of the resistance.

I hesitate when I get to Hunter's pallet, unsure of the protocol or what he'll allow. If we were home, he'd open his arms and wings and snuggle me into his chest. I'd fall asleep to the steady thud of his heart and be woken by his feverish kisses and questing hands.

A lump stoppers my throat but I refuse to cry under the

disdainful gaze of the Protectorate.

There must be other sleeping quarters. There are thousands of angels remaining despite our rebellion. Do the other non-angel varieties of the Protectorate have their own ships? Are there just as many of them? Even that show of force seems like nothing against the sheer scale of *one* universe.

Maybe there are millions of them. Maybe resistance really is futile.

Hunter narrows his eyes at me standing over him. I fall to my knees, bruising them on the floor in my haste. I drop my gaze to my hands on my thighs instead of staring at him.

Submissive. I can be submissive. Best not to provoke his dominance or appear to be challenging him. I can't beat him in the arena. I have to beat him out here, find something that will trigger the real Hunter and overwhelm the collar. Maybe I can wait until he's sleeping and unfasten the damn thing.

I smother a snort. Sure. The second I move, he'll be awake and aware. He's the lightest sleeper I know—when he's not in a healing coma.

Excitement tingles. *That's it.* I need to get him alone and unresponsive in a healing coma in Bronwyn's ward. Then I can get that bloody collar off him.

Which, unfortunately, takes me back to the arena and the fact I can't hurt him. Don't want to hurt him. But if it means freeing him...

"This is a human token, yes?"

His voice snaps me from my thoughts. My head jerks up. Hunter rolls his wedding ring between his finger and thumb. He flicks it at me and the band strikes my cheek, stinging before it bounces between my knees. I slap a hand down to keep it from tumbling away.

Hunter's lip curls. "Like you, it is useless and means nothing."

I flinch.

It's not him. *It's not him, it's not him.*

The words offer little comfort against the stab of pain.

I curl on my side, my back to Hunter. His wedding ring bites into my palm. I'm clenching my fist around it. Tears burn but I stare at the floor without blinking to keep them from falling. I slip the band onto my thumb and twist it, around and around and around.

I think about our wedding. His promise of love and protection. Forever and always. The heat in his eyes. The solidness of his body when he tugged me against him.

The lights click off and plunge the sleeping quarters into darkness since there are no windows to the stars in this depressing box. My harsh breathing is too loud. My blood roars in my ears. I strain to listen, to see anything but black. A whimper flutters in my throat but I clamp my teeth before it can escape.

The angels can see while I'm blind. Are they watching me trembling in the dark? Will they pounce now that the lights are out? Will Hunter?

I inch closer to him. A warning growl trickles from behind me. My heart is the only thing that's not frozen, hammering against my ribs.

Every sigh, every slither, is a warrior angel creeping through the blackness.

Is Hunter keeping me in suspense to prolong my punishment? I've been brought to him. He can do whatever he wants to me. Or is he worried that sex will provoke the real Hunter? Maybe he's been battling for control this entire time. There's no other reason for him not to rape me, as is his right as the dominant.

Time passes, marked by my slowing pulse until some noise sends it bounding again. Adrenaline spikes and drains, leaving me jittery and exhausted. Shutting my eyes makes no difference to the unrelieved dark. My shoulder and hip ache against the solid floor. Pins and needles nibble at my arm, worsened by my shivering.

Sleep snatches at me but leaves me more tired rather than less. My eyes are gritty. I can hear each blink. I jerk awake every few minutes or hours, convinced fingers are about to grab me and pin me down. To hurt and bruise. To take.

The chill sinks into my bones, the space somehow not heated by the proximity of so many warrior angels. A shudder grinds my sore body into the ground.

I shut my eyes. They may already be shut. When I open them again seconds later, the lights are on, bathing everything in a gentle, golden glow. Hunter's breath stirs my hair. I've cuddled into his chest in my sleep. One wing flops over me like a warm, weighted blanket. His lashes brush his sharp cheekbones, his face relaxed. Unguarded. Beautiful.

His eyes open. Midnight-blue. Dark, dilated pupils.

I hold my breath.

Hunter blinks once.

And smashes the solid heel of his hand into my ribs.

15

Hunter's strike shoots me across the floor, and I collide with another angel. She grunts in disgust and kicks me away. I flop on my front, too stunned to cry out. Breathing feels like knives are being slid between my ribs. Footsteps thud. I turn my face and press my cheek to the cold ground. At this angle, Hunter's laced boots stride for the door. The angel who kicked me is still lying on her side, watching me with glittering eyes.

They're all watching me.

I scramble to my feet, unable to smother a whimper at the sharp grind of bone in my chest. Hungry anticipation shivers amongst the Protectorate.

Hunter exits through the lower doorway of the sleeping quarters, not bothering to look back. I clutch my ribs, and stagger after him. My tortured breathing shortens further as the warrior angels stalk nearer on all fours, narrowing my escape route. The angels above perch on the edge of their floating pallets like birds of prey tracking a mouse in the grass. Ready to shred its delicate flesh to strips of meat and blood.

Uziyah stays on his bed, his expression giving me nothing while his brethren pour around him, closer and closer to hemming me in. My heart stabs against my shattered ribs with each frantic beat.

I'm running by the time I reach the door. Fingertips graze my shoulder, my ankle. A tug rips a clump of hair from my scalp. Tears burn my eyes. Half-blind, I lurch down the corridor until my vision sparkles to white and forces me to slow.

"Hunter," I wheeze.

He disappears around a corner. I manage two steps then brace my hand on the wall at a wave of dizziness. I jerk my head to look behind me, white fizzing to black and threatening to buckle my knees. The corridor is empty, the sleeping quarters out of sight. I rest my cold forehead on the colder wall. Tiny sips of air scorch my lungs.

If I chase after Hunter, I'll collapse. I need Bronwyn's healing shroud and gentle hands. She's the only one who's gentle.

A sob nearly finishes me in a brilliant burst of pain. I gasp and stagger onwards, trying to remember the reverse of the path Uziyah took yesterday. Every bloody corridor looks the same.

Angels swoop past me, and I cower. They sneer or scoff but flap on their way. No Creators cross my route. Maybe Salam, Tallai and Bronwyn are the full complement needed onboard. It's not like the angels are disobedient.

Not anymore.

I lose my sense of direction, though I had none to begin with. Agony lances my side. It gets harder and harder to breathe. Terror floods copper into my mouth. Or my ribs have pierced a lung.

What if I stop breathing? Chest filled with blood, my brain bereft of oxygen. No one cares enough to carry me to the healing ward. They'll leave me crumpled on the floor, slowly turning blue. Too far gone for the Creators' medical marvels to fix me.

My shoulder slides along the wall—the only thing keeping me upright. Air rattles in my lungs and burns like acid. My eyes struggle to focus. The corridor stretches on and on to the infinity of space, narrowing to blackness. Nothingness. Death.

I wish I could have hugged Steph one more time. Inhaled her comforting scent of Parma Violets and jasmine. Listened to Greg prattle on about whatever subject excited him that day.

I wish I could have saved us all. But I can't even save myself.

The solid surface vanishes from under my shoulder. I list into the void, and topple, slamming onto my side.

I manage a single, piercing shriek.

Then I faint.

* * *

Heat sinks into my chilled and broken bones. My ribs expand, fighting a constriction, though there's no pain. My lids flutter, the lashes stuck together. It's too much effort to peel my eyes open.

I'm safe and warm. Healed. I want to stay here.

I've never been hurt like this, not even during the apocalypse. Nothing more than bruises. I hadn't broken a bone until Hunter snapped my arm between his hands.

I flinch on my slab and squeeze my eyes shut tighter. My fists clench but I force them to relax, not wanting to alert Bronwyn that I'm awake. I steady my breathing. The hush of the room remains unchanged. I crack open one bleary eye.

Pink liquid ripples in the tank, stirred by a phantom wind. A humming noise increases from the corridor. I let my muscles go floppy, keeping one lid slitted enough to see. A stretcher floats into the healing ward, bearing the shattered form of Uziyah curled on his side. Bones poke through feathers. A knee and an elbow bend the wrong way.

How long have I been here? He was fine and whole when I left the sleeping quarters. But I guess that means nothing on this ship of nightmares.

His teeth are gritted, his ash-grey irises the only colour left in his face. Bronwyn guides the stretcher to the slab he occupied before. Uziyah painfully shimmies onto the pallet, his jaw bulging at each movement. Sweat glistens on his bare and battered torso.

"I will set your bones and then you may sleep," Bronwyn says.

Uziyah offers a weak nod. She wraps her long fingers around his lower leg and tucks his foot under her armpit. Her wings flare. She yanks, and his joint cracks. My heart thumps at his low groan. I shut my eye. Of course, it doesn't drown out Uziyah's grunts or the grating slide of bone. My limbs ache in sympathy.

Did Hunter do this? Some kind of rematch? Or are the others challenging him after his fall from grace, like I predicted?

"Sit up now." Bronwyn's voice is calm but detached. A doctor with her patient.

There's a rustle. A grind of teeth and a hiss of breath. A whine—quickly smothered. The hush creeps back into the space. I peek again. Bronwyn finishes wrapping dressings around Uziyah's splinted wings, his feathers ruffled and dull.

"Rest," she says.

She leaves him sitting on the edge of the slab and bustles

from the room. The pad of her steps fades down the corridor. Uziyah bows his head, his body criss-crossed by bandages. His right arm is strapped to his chest. Sunflower-yellow hair spills over his slumped shoulders and brushes his thighs, the colour too cheery for the dejected angel it belongs to.

I untangle myself from the healing shroud and creep to the tank, remembering my last attempt to make him an ally.

"Uziyah?" I whisper.

Nothing—not even a twitch.

I say his name louder. He raises his head. His eyes are bleak and dark with despair. Then he blinks, each lid out of sync, and his expression drains to wariness and exhaustion.

"Fee-feeble creature," he slurs. "You live. That is—a surprise."

Another sluggish blink. He sways.

Jesus Christ, there's clear fluid leaking out of his ears. Can warrior angels heal a brain injury?

He really should lie down.

"Who did this?"

Steph would ask me why I care and I wouldn't be able to answer. Actually, no, she wouldn't need to ask. She knows I'm a bleeding heart when it comes to wounded creatures. Even wounded arseholes, it seems.

"Hunter." Uziyah gives a harsh laugh. "To prove—it was no fluke."

I wince. My feet shuffle forward. Uziyah appears not to notice, his gaze unfocused and drifting.

Hunter was prickly to start with. Suspicious. But all he needed was kindness and affection to dissolve his stony exterior. Maybe Uziyah will be the same.

And if he's not, if he breaks me into little pieces, I guess there's no better place to be than the healing ward.

I swallow my nerves, my mouth dry. One step. Another. I suck in a breath. Uziyah stares at his knee. The swollen flesh stretches the loose material of his trousers.

Before I can think about what a terrible idea this is, I hug him. He's so broad, my arms don't go all the way around.

Now, he twitches.

"What—what are you doing?"

His one good arm flaps at me. The heat of his skin bakes through my bodysuit. He smells like the sea.

"I'm comforting you," I say firmly. "It's what friends do when one of them has had a bad day."

"I do not need—I do not…"

The fight leaches out of him. I wobble under his bulk.

"Okay," I say, my voice strained, "time to lie down."

He manages to swing one leg up onto the slab. I hoist the other, and my spine cracks.

Bloody hell, he weighs as much as a tree. I'm surprised he can fly. Hunter is a feather compared to him.

Uziyah rolls drunkenly onto his good side to face the wall. His body goes limp. I watch the steady rise and fall of his ribs beneath the splinted wings.

He probably won't remember the hug when he wakes in a few days. Or it'll piss him off and he'll make me regret it.

I turn back to my bed slab. Bronwyn lingers in the doorway, her hands tucked to her concave chest.

"You show him compassion when he has only treated you with disdain." She cocks her head to peer at me out of one navy and amethyst eye. "Why?"

"Because you've made sure all he knows is violence. I want him to see there's another way to live. A way that doesn't depend on aggression and cruelty. The way Hunter chose."

I stalk to my bed and stretch out on my back, frowning at the ceiling, my arms crossed.

If Bronwyn wants me to leave, she can drag me out.

"Uziyah is aggressive because he was built that way, child. The cybernetics in his brain ensure it."

"Maybe all he needs is one person to be nice to him." I hug my arms tighter. "Maybe your technology is not as infallible as you think it is. You already made a mistake with their vulnerability to iron."

She gives me a look. "Creators do not make mistakes. The Protectorate have been modelled on our physiology, though enhanced. We can build our tools to have rapid healing but we cannot manufacture it in ourselves. That is what our technology is for."

So the Creators have a similar physiology to the angels. Not the super-sealing or semi-invincibility but the reaction to iron. They'll all turn to yellow froth if I shove a blade in their guts.

I need to get the knife off of Hunter. The one I hid on him when we were attacked in the church. It's a weapon and a bargaining chip. The only slice of power I have, unless I can get my hands on the iron swords from the arena, though I bet those are better protected than the weapon forgotten in Hunter's boot.

"Even your technology can glitch and break," I say, still frowning at the ceiling. "All we need—all Hunter needs—is a chance."

"Hunter was defective, child. Uziyah is not."

"You made Hunter that way."

"We were experimenting. It was a failure."

"He's a living, feeling, intelligent creature just like you, for fuck's sake."

Bronwyn flinches. "He is a… tool."

"Do you really believe that or do you just parrot what Salam and Tallai say?"

She's silent for over a minute. Then, finally, a soft, "It does not matter what I believe."

"Of course it does. What we do and think matters. Hunter matters"—my breath hitches—"and I'll get him back."

Cool fingers caress my forehead.

"Perhaps you should worry about yourself, child," Bronwyn says quietly, "and not what you have lost."

Well, at least it's a little different than being told to take my punishment with grace.

She turns away before I can respond, leaving me alone with the comatose Uziyah. I shut my eyes and fall asleep to the gentle sigh of his breaths.

16

A few days pass. I think. Time is marked by when the warrior angels are awake and when they're asleep, not by the sun or the moon. The brightest star in this universe is a blue-white ball glimpsed through a window with some kind of comfort shield. The nearest planet is a globe of green and gold, its five moons much smaller. An assortment of space-faring vessels zip to and fro, as orderly as traffic on a motorway.

I don't sleep. Nights are for shivering fear, waiting for someone to kill me and hoping I don't move too close to Hunter in my tiny bursts of unconsciousness. Days are for trailing after him like a shadow, and more fear. Fear of being left alone. I'm too scared to even explore the ship and get my bearings or find something that might help me save Hunter.

The angels are always watching and every gaze holds the promise of violence.

Hunter ignores me. I pretend it doesn't hurt. I take comfort in every hour he doesn't touch me. If he were the Creators' Hunter, he would have raped me by now.

I worry about Steph and Greg. How they're being treated. If they're getting enough to eat. The only food is the tart drink from the shuttle, dished out every few rotations of sleep and not-sleep. It must be working because I don't feel hungry in between. I'm also not producing any waste so lord knows what it's doing to my insides.

My plan of getting Hunter injured enough to send him to the healing ward is not going well. I can't get close to grab the iron knife sticking out of his boot. The thought of jamming it in his ribs makes me nauseated. I felt bad after doing it even when he was an enemy.

He also never loses a challenge. He's ruthless. Brutal. Breaking wings and slicing deep. I shut my eyes when he claims his victory.

Maybe there are different rules for dominating if the defeated falls unconscious. Hunter's victims are always awake. I'm the only one who wasn't. Is that why he hasn't claimed me? Or maybe I'm no longer what he wants.

I'm not allowed to follow him when Salam or Tallai take him into a private room. The first time, I glimpsed a raised bed and no other furniture. I yelled at Salam. Hunter growled and raised his hand to strike me. Salam gave me a wicked, sharp-beaked grin as he slowly shut the door in my face. I heaved in the corridor, nothing coming up but sour bile and drool.

My Hunter hated servicing his creators.

This time, I sit with my back to the wall, knees to chest so I'm as unobtrusive as possible. I press my hands over my ears though I never hear anything from within the room. Maybe it's insulated. Or maybe the act is as mechanical as it sounds.

My Hunter always made a bit of noise when he was enjoying himself.

I swipe at a tear. The door hisses open and Hunter glides out, not looking at me, his expression proud and smugly satisfied. My stomach clenches. I scrabble to my feet and walk in his wake.

"Hunter," Salam says from behind us.

I slam to a stop to avoid running into Hunter's back. We turn, though only I glare at the Creator. Salam treats me to a disdainful brow arch. His knobbly fingers smooth the arms and legs of his bodysuit.

"She is not suffering enough," he says.

Hunter fixes his gaze on me, all dark eyes and cheekbones. "She will suffer."

His wings stretch, filling the corridor. My heart drops to my bare feet.

"Make sure she does." Salam stalks away.

Hunter stares at me for a second more. When he spins on his heel, I force myself to keep up despite the reluctance screaming in my joints.

He leads us to a wide room where the Protectorate train and exercise, weapons and machines spread throughout. The space is almost empty, a group of five huddled in one corner. Their voices reach us, though they don't seem to have noticed our entrance.

"You are an embarrassment, Uziyah," the white-haired female says. The one who wanted to carve my flesh. She shoves the bulkier angel against the wall. "You should be ashamed to show your face."

He must have been released from the healing ward today. What does he remember?

The brown-haired, brown-eyed male who wanted to 'take me', leans his forearm on Uziyah's throat and gets in his face. "You lost to Hunter again, and Hunter is weak. That means you are weaker. Perhaps I will go next. It is my turn to get what I want."

"So challenge Hunter." My voice echoes in the room. I find myself striding between the machines to stand in front of the warriors mocking Uziyah. I plant my hands on my hips. "If you're so confident Hunter is weak, challenge him yourself. See if you do better."

The angel's eyes flick to Hunter. A sneer quickly masks the flash of uncertainty.

"We have all had Hunter on his knees."

Hunter smirks. It's not the smirk I'm used to—smouldering and sexy. It's taunting. Cruel.

"Show me, Riot," he growls. "Show me what it is like to kneel, for I have forgotten."

The male angel—Riot—swallows hard. He glances at the female. Hunter tracks his gaze. His smirk morphs to a cold smile.

"Abayankari," he says, "some things I have not forgotten."

The final three warriors ease away from Uziyah, Riot and Abayankari. They trot from the room.

Abayankari sticks her chin in the air. "That collar may have improved your confidence and your attitude, *Hunter,* but you are still weak."

"Then challenge me," he purrs.

Abayankari's chin gets so high, I'm surprised she doesn't tip over backwards.

"We challenge," she spits.

Riot's wings flare, his face carefully neutral. Abayankari's head snaps towards him, swinging her white hair in an arc.

"We challenge," Riot says, though even I can hear the hesitation.

The trio stalk from the room, leaving Uziyah and me alone. He slumps against the wall. His skin is still pale and dull after his healing coma.

"Are you all—"

"Why must you interfere?" he sighs.

"I was trying to help—"

"Do not help. You do not help." He shoves himself upright and clenches his fists. "Help from you only makes me look weaker."

I sidle around to put some kind of weight contraption between us. I get brave enough to glower at the stubborn arse.

"Hunter didn't complain when I offered to protect him. He took it for what it was—a sign that I cared."

"Why would you care? I am no coupler of humans."

I hear the ghost of the words—*moally tumsasha*—beneath the translation.

Human fucker.

I roll my eyes. "I don't want to have sex with you, Uziyah. I'm married. I'm just trying to be your friend."

Maybe if I say it enough, he'll give in.

He limps past me, sparing a scowl at the rings on my left hand. I curl my fingers around them. His limp is absent when he reaches the door, though his back is stiff.

"You cling to human customs but you are the only human here. None of it will help you. I cannot..." He snaps his teeth. "I *will not* help you."

I open my mouth to tell him I'm not the only human but he stomps through the door, his wings arched. He disappears around a bend.

He must think I'm not watching—think I can't stalk him on silent feet—because when he seems to believe he's alone, his wings droop and his limp returns.

17

Something is wrong.

I blink awake. Unease churns in my stomach, and goose-bumps prickle my arms from the cold floor.

Hunter's bed pallet is empty.

I roll onto my back. Angels loom over me in silence. Triumph twists their faces.

"No!" I yelp.

I scramble upright. My shoulders hit the wall. The warriors trap me in a semi-circle.

No sign of Hunter. No Uziyah. The angels are a mix of the golden and white winged, plus our Jewels.

I remember all their names. We took them to dinner on one of their first proper nights with us after they were released from government detention. Showed them human hospitality beyond suspicious scientists and sharp tools. Steph and I nearly died from laughter at the confusion on their faces when we went to a club and they were confronted with swirling lights, shimmying bodies and a heavy beat. But after we got some alcohol in them, the warrior angels were happy to shake their booties on the dance floor.

A male steps closer. He has ruby wings and curly, brown hair.

He hugged me when I invited him to my wedding. Hunter had to peel him off with a growl of, "Mine." Angels don't cry—they don't have the anatomy for it—but Markian's eyes held gratitude and happiness.

Now, they're flat and cold. A collar glows on his throat.

He backhands me. The blow flares hot pain in my jaw and spins me around. My palms slap the wall. The heat of many bodies closes in.

Surrounded. Mobbed.

I whirl to face a row of bared teeth and rustling wings. Nowhere to run. I block a second slap, twisting the wrist and driving Markian back. He trips and vanishes into the throng. Hard hands pinch and shove and jostle. My foot slams between the legs of another male. He crumples. A second takes his place. I duck a punch. Return my own. My knuckles burst on a perfect jaw.

There are too many of them. I fight, but I'm a fragile human in a semi-invincible world.

My ribs break again. My cheekbone—that's new. The familiar taste of blood coats my mouth. Fists pummel soft flesh.

Bearing the trauma isn't easier despite knowing I won't die from it. Probably. Bronwyn will patch my body together then send me back out to be beaten. Again and again and again until my mind can't take it anymore.

The angels batter me in silence. My cries echo in the sleeping quarters until the ringing in my ears drowns them out. Shock and pain stun my senses.

I'm on the ground. There's a dull tearing in my gut when I breathe.

A boot connects with my stomach.

I can't breathe anymore.

"Enough," a voice says.

Maybe Uziyah. It's difficult to focus beyond the buzzing, shrieking agony of my body. My eyes are blurred and swimming in red. Everything is red.

"Her torment is Hunter's," Uziyah continues.

Was he always here? Was he the one who stamped on my hand and snapped all my fingers? He said I'd pay for his defeat.

"What business is it of yours?" a female says. "Hunter left her to suffer."

"The Creators decreed her punishment is to suffer and heal until she breaks. She has suffered. Now, I will take her to be healed. Perhaps later, she will break."

Not exactly a comforting speech on my behalf. Is his insistence on following the letter of their law a pretence? If he wanted me to pay, all he had to do was nothing. I doubt the healing bath would piece together my skull and brain after a few stomps to the head.

Careful hands scoop me off the floor. I think they're trying to be gentle but everywhere hurts. A whine shivers out of my throat. My breaths come in tortured gasps.

They hurt, too.

"You are not what you once were to command us so, Uziyah. When you return, I will challenge."

A flinch transfers from the broad chest pressed to my side.

"And I will accept," Uziyah says stiffly.

The ground spins. Or we spin. Dizziness and nausea swirl from my brain to my gut and back again. The vibration of Uziyah's steps grinds my bones together. Muscles flex against me. The crimson haze in my vision remains, broken only by the smudge of passing lights in the ceiling far above. Uziyah boosts me higher in his arms. Pain crackles in my nervous system. My whimper sounds loud even over the rush of my pulse in my ears.

I have Uziyah's hair gripped in my fist. A huge rope of it. When did that happen? It tugs through my hand, and I tighten my aching fingers. I'm basically pulling his hair.

He mutters, "Foolish, feeble creature."

"I knew… we could be friends," I manage to wheeze.

"We are not friends."

He grumbles the words but there's no heat. No anger. Just stubborn and sulky. A hulking contrarian.

Maybe he's mellowing.

"Thank you, Uziyah," I whisper. "For saving me."

"Do not thank me. You are tiny and weak yet make everything worse."

My snort is a brief, rib-shattering puff of air. "You make it worse—for yourselves. You let… the Creators… do anything just because they built you. They're an abusive parent you need to cut—from your life."

The effort of speaking leaves me woozy. I sag in Uziyah's hold, red turning to black as my eyes slip shut.

Uziyah tuts. "You know nothing."

"I know you're isolated and lost. Just like Hunter was."

My voice fades. Everything fades.

Except for a slightly worried, "Feeble creature?" then a quiet, tentative, "Maia?"

18

"You have ten minutes," Uziyah snaps.

He spares a sneer for Steph and Greg through the dwindling gap of their cell door as it slides shut, sealing us three humans inside. Steph glares right back, her brown hair frizzed in indignation.

"Still an arsehole, I see," she says.

I ponder the entrance as if I can watch Uziyah's bulky figure stomp away on the other side.

He collected me from Bronwyn's care. I remember him carrying me in the corridor but nothing else until I woke up, once again bathed in pink goo. I expected him to be on his slab, broken from his latest challenge, but he appeared in the doorway, greeting me with a mulish expression and monosyllables. And he brought me here. To my friends.

I doubt that was a command from the Creators.

I must be getting through to him. *I must be*. Letting me see my friends is an act of mercy. It gives me hope. There's no way he'd allow that without mellowing.

Unless crushing it will be all the sweeter later.

No. I can't think like that. I've been cut too deep already. I can't take another slice.

"I think his bark is worse than his bite," I say, still facing the door.

Greg snorts. "Oh, he'll bite all right. And what even is ten minutes in this fucking place? I never thought I'd get bored of being on a spaceship yet here we are."

I manage a smile. Warmth flickers in my chest. I've been feeling so hollow. So weak and useless. Whenever I leave the healing ward, it's like the shroud or the bath has stolen another little part of me.

There wasn't much to begin with. What happens when I have nothing left?

I shake off the sucking, sinking sensation and turn to my friends. Steph leans on Greg, her hand tucked into his elbow. Her eyes widen.

"Jesus, Maia!" she gasps. "What have those bastards done to you?"

I glance down at myself. My bodysuit is even more tattered after my latest pummelling. It's worse off than the battle-scarred remnants of the wedding dress she last saw me in.

"Not what you're wearing—your face!" She relinquishes her grip on Greg and limps two steps to cup my chin. "You've lost weight. You're practically gaunt, and your eyes…"

"What's wrong with my eyes?"

Her gaze flits across my face. Greg's worried expression churns in my gut.

"You look kinda shocky, Maia," he whispers.

Steph gathers me against her chest in a waft of Parma Violets and jasmine. Her heart thuds beneath the silk of her bridesmaid's dress.

"You don't smell," I mutter for some reason.

Her strangled noise vibrates into my ear. "Nice of you to notice. Greg doesn't smell, either."

She squeezes me tighter. Greg's arms circle me from behind, his frame stocky and comforting at my back. He's only a head taller than me. He usually smells like weed but it seems to have faded without access to his stash.

"Greg smells like biscuits," I say to Steph's boob.

She makes the strangled noise again. My cheek is pressed so close to her, I feel the hitch of her ribs.

"Stop sniffing us and tell me what the hell they've done to you," she says, anguished. "I'll kill them. I'll fucking kill them."

"They're teaching me my lesson."

My voice is empty. My eyes are burning but dry despite the pain grinding my insides. Steph strokes my hair, likely stroking Greg alongside. He mumbles soothing nonsense into my scalp.

They're the only thing holding me together. Without them, I'd drift off into space like a piece of flotsam.

"They're using Hunter to hurt me."

Okay, the tonelessness is starting to freak me out. I thought I was doing good. Coping. But infinity yawns beneath my feet, ready to swallow me. How insignificant and futile my struggles are against the vastness of the universe. The *universes*.

"It's not him. Don't ever forget that, Maia—it's not him. He would never hurt you. If he were here, there wouldn't be enough left of the Creators to scrape into a beaker."

But he's not here.

I sway in Steph and Greg's hold.

"Maybe we should sit down," Greg says.

We hobble as one entity towards the window. I stare at my reflection glowing in the blue-white blaze of the sun.

Gaunt is right. Shadows fill my sunken cheeks and rim my sockets. My hair hangs thin and limp and tangled, though clean from the healing bath. My collarbones and ribs are harsh lines through the rents in my bodysuit. I drop my gaze instead of meeting eyes that are too wide, too bright.

I swallow hard. And again. My throat clicks.

"The angels don't get a window," I croak. "They sleep in a huge square room with floating pallets. It's pitch black when the lights go out."

Steph tuts. "Of course you still worry about the angels. My little bleeding heart."

"Lucky pricks," Greg says. "It barely gets dark here. The sun is always shining. It's driving me nuts, man."

Steph flicks his arm, both of us leaning on him. "It's not that bad. Things could clearly be worse for us."

"Sure, I know. Sorry, Maia. But we're Scottish. This much sunlight is unnatural."

The ghost of a smile tugs at my mouth. Steph and Greg cradle me between them and we slide down the wall in an ungainly pile beneath the window. The sun casts a rectangle of light on the floor beyond our feet. Greg's still wearing his dress shoes, though the toes are scuffed.

My friends cuddle me as if they're afraid I might shatter.

And I might.

"Keep talking," I say, resting my head on Steph's shoulder. "I want to hear about you two. I don't want to think of anything outside this room. Not for… not for however long we have left."

I don't want to go back out there. I want to stay here where it's safe and calm with Steph and Greg. Where people hug me, not hurt me.

My breath wobbles, fractures. Speeds.

Steph manages to nudge Greg despite the buffer of my

shuddering body between them. Crap, when did my teeth start chattering? Panic curls in my throat.

I'm really not okay.

"We, uh… so the, um, planet," Greg says, shimmying closer until he's pressed shoulder to hip. "Our ship is in geosynchronous orbit with it. I don't know what a day is in this universe but it takes 216,000 seconds to change from night to day on the surface. I counted Mississippily and everything."

"Yeah, cause that wasn't annoying," Steph says under her breath.

"That's two-and-a-half times longer than an Earth day, which is 86,400 seconds," Greg continues, unfazed. "I obviously haven't been counting constantly—"

"Which is why your testicles are still intact," Steph says.

"—but…" Greg coughs, his cheeks flushed, "I've extrapolated that we've been stuck here for eight Creator days, or twenty of our days."

My heart thuds. *Twenty days!* How much time have I spent unconscious?

"The answer to your unspoken question, and I presume all the sniffing, is we don't smell because we have one of those hidden panel rooms that's some kind of weird cleaning tube," Steph says.

Greg bounces beside me. "It's a total trip, man. You stand inside and this hot air blasts over you, rippling your clothes. It sucks out all the dirt and shit."

Steph laughs, though it's a little forced. "Not actual shit."

Greg's cheeks pink. "No, but on that… Is anyone else freaked out they haven't been for a piss in twenty days? That can't be healthy."

"None of this is healthy."

Greg chuckles. "Right, true. Not to even mention the amount of alien microbes we've been exposed to."

Steph pinches the flesh between Greg's thumb and index finger.

They're holding hands across my lap. When did that happen? Their other hands are clasped around mine, all of us cold. Their shoulders prop me up.

I raise my gaze. "Are you two…?"

They look at each other over the top of my head. I never knew Greg blushed so easily.

"We're not cheating or anything," Steph says quickly. "There's not much else to do but talk and keep each other warm. Greg's been really supportive."

Greg wiggles his eyebrows. "Literally and figuratively."

Steph slaps him on the knuckles, though her smile is fond. Greg grins at her, and even I can see the adoration in it.

This is what I needed—a reminder of what I'm fighting for. My two best friends growing closer but not yet complete. They need their third. I need my other half. The Creators don't get to ruin that. They don't get to win.

I sit up straighter, startling Steph and Greg. Their hands fly to my shoulders as if they're worried I'm about to keel over.

"I'll get him back," I say, my voice stronger. Less hollow and frightening. "I'll get Devinon back. For both of you."

Greg splutters. "He's not mine to get back. I don't need…"

Steph cocks an eyebrow at him.

"Fine," Greg sighs. "Maybe I miss the big, blue lug."

Steph squeezes his hand. "I'll tell him you said that, prickly pear."

Greg pouts. "Shut up."

Steph and I share a laugh at his expense. Like old times. It clears the last of the fug from my brain. I cuddle them both, giving them each a sloppy, smacking kiss on the cheek.

"I love you guys," I say, a catch in my throat. "I'll get us out of this."

"We never doubted it for a second, Maia," Steph says. "We love you, too."

Greg's head bobs. "We only wish we could help. Get us out of this room and we'll storm the spaceship like we stormed Edinburgh Castle. *Nemo me impune lacessit.*"

"Damn fucking right no one provokes us with impunity," Steph hisses, her teeth bared in a feral smile.

Steph and Greg share a high-five above my head. I beam at them, lighter than I've been in days.

The door glides open while we're hugging and slapping each other on the back. We freeze, all in a tangle. Uziyah's cool and sooty eyes sweep over us. His face is blank. Calculating or curious? He blinks, and his lip lifts into a disjointed sneer, as if he's having trouble remembering his favourite expression.

We lever ourselves upright under his stare. Steph winces and rubs her hip. A blip of guilt tumbles to my gut. I spin to Uziyah.

"Let me take Steph to the healing ward—she's in pain." I hesitate for a beat. "Please?"

I can't believe I didn't think of it before. She's been suffering without her medication and mobility aids. Flare ups no doubt triggered by all the stress of alien abduction. The shroud might not be sophisticated enough to cure degenerative and autoimmune conditions but it should ease her pain, for a while at least. Not that she needs a cure. As she likes to say—she's awesome as she is. To be abled would be too much for the universe to handle.

"Don't ask him for anything, Maia," she says. "It's not worth it. And he won't understand, big tough fruit bat that he is."

Uziyah glowers at Steph.

"Oh, he understands pain," I say softly.

His eyes widen a fraction then he schools his expression to haughty indifference.

"I cannot take your—"

"Best friend," I say helpfully.

"—weak human to the healing ward." Uziyah fixes me with a glare when I open my mouth to protest. "Not yet."

Steph nudges me. "What did he say?"

I'm so used to the instant translation, I forget it's there, the angel's language a pleasant backdrop beneath it.

"He says he can't take you yet. Why not?" I direct at Uziyah.

"Ask him if he can get us some of the translating nanotech," Greg whispers.

I roll my eyes. "He can understand and speak English, Greg. You know that already."

"I'm losing my edge in this stupid box," Greg huffs.

Uziyah's gaze stays on me throughout the exchange, impenetrable and unshifting.

"The Creators have a surprise for you," he says.

Oh, brilliant.

More cruelty.

19

I've never been in this room before. It's a squat amphitheatre, the oval floor bordered by a smooth wall that slopes to a single viewing platform. The rear wall curves to the ceiling and funnels into a shaft in the centre—the only way to access the space. Uziyah carries me into this new, nightmarish room. Not how he carried me to the healing ward, but under his arm like a sack of potatoes.

He plonks me on my feet on the platform and stands behind me, hulking over my shoulder. Salam and Tallai range in front, and survey their warriors in the oval below. Salam keeps glancing at me over his leathery wing. Satisfaction burns in his violet and violent eyes. He drinks in my torn bodysuit and weight loss with the thirst of a hummingbird in the desert.

I want to punch his beak in.

I inch closer to Uziyah. The heat of him bakes my spine.

"Be still, feeble creature," he hisses.

If I were a less confident person, I'd question whether I was really getting through to him. But he's definitely the lesser of many evils in this place.

"Come forward, human." Salam gestures with an impatient sweep of his two-thumbed hand. "I want you to witness."

I totter three steps on wobbling legs. Four rows of five

angels glare up at me, Hunter alone in his own row at the front, Devinon behind him. Collars circle every throat. The malevolent light burnishes jewel-bright feathers and gilds the dark arch of bows slung across backs. Markian attempts to kill me with the power of his eyeballs. My cheek stings from the memory of his slap.

"Watch," Salam says, as if I'm not already watching.

A spindly finger swipes across the device on his wrist. In perfect, gut-clenching synchrony, twenty-one warriors reach for the collars around their necks. Then twenty-one collars clunk to the floor.

But their hatred remains unchanged.

"What…?" I croak.

Salam flashes his sharp teeth. "The collar was not simply a means of control. It is too unwieldy for our fine weapons to be burdened with long term. We would not want to risk their battle prowess."

Another swipe. Twenty-one angels leap into the air, filling the cramped space with the clatter of wings. Their bows appear in their hands, strings drawn tight. Blue-tipped arrows start to sing their awful song, and all my body fluids dry up in fear.

One command—one swipe—and I'm a glorified porcupine. Then dust.

"The collar provides temporary control while it enhances the cybernetics already in their brains," Salam says, the buzz of his words dimmer than the anxiety floating around my skull. "The cybernetics have now grown to the same extent as the rest of the Protectorate. The way it would have been had we not chosen to experiment. But we, too, have lessons to learn."

I force my numb lips to move. "What does that mean?"

Salam taps his wrist. I scramble backwards, trip over my

feet and fall on my arse, rattling my teeth together. Salam and Tallai cackle at me. Hunter and the other twenty warriors settle into their neat rows, no change in expression to show they're disappointed at not being allowed to shoot me full of arrows. No sign of anything beyond the glitter of their eyes.

"It means, human, that the collars have performed the function we gave them." Salam tilts his head, his bony crest tilting it further. "Did you truly think it would be as easy as removing the collar to return Hunter to the weak and submissive specimen he was before? You humans and your pathetic hope. Hunter will never be that way again."

I can't seem to get off my arse. Can't seem to take a full breath, either.

Getting close to Hunter to remove the collar was challenge enough. How am I supposed to fix his brain? How am I supposed to fix any of this?

I waited too long. I didn't try hard enough. Fight hard enough.

The sucking, gaping hole returns to yawn right under my feet.

"Hunter, you have been assigned a private room for the rest of the human's punishment. You will soon see why I ordered you to wait. Now you can do with her as you would any prize." Salam tents his fingers in the hollow of his concave chest. Righteous triumph sparks in his eyes. "And that will be the end of it."

The end of the punishment or the end of me? I guess there's no fucking difference.

I scuttle a retreat and bump into Uziyah's legs. I twist onto my knees, pleading up at him. Something flits through his eyes. Something like pity.

"Uziy-*aah—*"

I'm yanked backwards, throttled by my bodysuit. My feet leave the platform to kick at nothing. A fist between my shoulder blades hoists me into the air. Material rips.

I'm going to fall out of my bodysuit, completely naked, to be raped by angels.

Black wings brush the edges of my vision not blinded by the tangle and sway of my own hair. The ground drops away. Smug and disinterested faces track our departure until they're swallowed by the smooth walls of the shaft in the ceiling. Feathers brush the sides with each heavy beat.

I stay frozen while my heart seizes in my throat and chokes me.

Corridors whoosh by. Turquoise and pearl. A glimpse of the sun and the distant gold and green planet through a window.

A tiny hysterical voice in my head wonders how Hunter knows where he's going. Or did Salam programme the directions right into his brain?

Up, down, sideways. My belly revolts and shoots bile into my mouth. It's as sour as their food.

The swirl of colour and wind finally halts. Hunter's boots hit the floor at the same time as my knees, his hand still scruffing the back of my bodysuit. A door glides open. Hunter drags me through it. I glimpse a square room, empty except for a wide slab topped by a pallet. My hair puffs around my face on each breath.

"Please, Hunter," I croak. "*Please* don't do this."

Hunter tosses me onto the bed.

20

The pallet is more cushioned than it looks in the brief second my hands and knees hit it. I roll and tumble off into the space between the slab and the wall. Hunter flaps his wings, stirring my hair, and leaps onto the bed. Dark eyes appraise me above the slash of his cheekbones. He lunges for me and I jerk away, wedging my shoulders in the corner.

Trapped with a dangerous creature.

We've been here—in my boiler cupboard in my flat in Martello Court. Pinned in the dark by a horny, arrogant angel. His exploring hands. Letting him do what he wanted.

Except this time, what he wants will shatter me.

"Kneel," he says in his soft and menacing voice.

"Wait." It comes out a wheeze. I say it again but it's no different.

Wheezier, even.

I hold up my hands, as if that will ward him off. My fingers shake as badly as my voice.

I lick my lips. "Not everything has to be taken by force."

Hunter cocks his head. The gesture almost has me bawling. Familiar yet totally alien.

"*Kneel*," he growls.

My knees hit the unyielding floor. My vision wobbles from

the heartbeat quivering through my entire body.

Hunter crowds closer. His fist clenches in my hair, and my scalp protests.

"Wait!" I yelp. "Let me do it. I'll do it. Just… don't force me."

His grip doesn't loosen. Strands of my hair ping free with tiny starbursts of pain. I place my hands on his thighs. He stops moving. His intense gaze brands the top of my head but I can't meet it. His face belongs to a stranger. If I look, I'll panic and try to run.

Then he'll catch me and do what he wants.

I stare at the criss-cross of laces on the crotch of his trousers until my eyes blur.

The only way I'm surviving this is if I take the lead. Show him how to be gentle. *Remind him.*

Fear sits like a hundred prickly pears in my stomach.

Hunter's hold tightens. I gasp, and move my hands, stroking the firm muscle of his thighs. Placating. My fingertips brush the handle of the iron knife in his boot. Terror has me hesitating.

I want to yank it out and bury it in his groin. Slash and stab as if he were nothing more than a rapist. A monster.

But he's Hunter. His body belongs to my Hunter. I've knelt at his feet a hundred times just to watch the delight and hunger in his eyes. The flutter of his lashes when I suck him into my mouth. The way he sighs my name like a prayer.

Tears clog my throat. I pick at the laced crotch instead of crying.

My hope was for nothing. He hasn't raped me because he was warring with the real Hunter. Or was worried about his control. He waited because he was told to.

I continue to rub his leg from hip to knee, touching the knife on each pass. The laces loosen under my fumbling fingers. His erection spills free to bob in front of my face. I make the mistake of meeting his eyes.

They're all pupil—dilated and black. Lust simmers in their depths but it's the lust for tearing and fucking and blood.

A whimper bubbles up but I clamp my teeth and swallow it down. It lodges in my throat like a fish bone.

Hunter is one prey noise away from ripping me apart.

Tears dampen the thighs of my bodysuit. My shudders sprinkle the floor with them.

Taking a beating was one thing but this—warping my memories of affection and intimacy with the horror of violence—is too much. Too awful.

I can't do it.

"Do something or I will do it for you," Hunter says.

My breath catches at the barely restrained hostility. Black wings arch, dwarfing everything and trapping me further. Muscles shift beneath my hands. His aggression tastes like pennies on my tongue. I grab for him, wrapping my fingers around his shaft and squeezing desperately.

He stills. His rage simmers between us.

I have to do this. I *can* do this. Give my husband a spectacular orgasm to remind him who he is. Show the Creators that love is stronger than their fucking technology.

Handjob only, though. Anything else is too risky.

I pump my hand. He likes firm pressure. A twist at the end. My thumb grazing the crown.

His eyes watch me, unblinking. Nerves swoop into my gut and jump around with all the goddamn cacti. He cants his hips. The hand gripping my skull guides me forward.

No way is he going in my mouth. He'll break my jaw worse

than Uziyah's.

I aim for a testicle instead. Roll it between my lips and lave it with my tongue, tugging gently. Finally, Hunter's lashes flutter closed for a second of reprieve, his head tipped back.

We discovered he enjoyed ball play when I got a little adventurous in the bath. His wings flared and soaked the whole room.

On my next stroke of his leg, I swipe the knife from his boot and stuff it under the pallet. My heart thuds loud enough to betray me. I ease onto my heels, too wired and twitchy to have his balls in my mouth.

Hunter straightens slowly. Black eyes glitter. He stoops and grabs my biceps, hoisting me aloft. My spine hits the wall. I manage a squeak. A forearm across my neck changes it to a gargle. Hunter yanks the bodysuit, dragging the stretchy material off my shoulders to bunch around my wrists and sag to my knees, exposing me in between. His bruising hand hooks my thigh over his hip. I shove and claw at his chest. His forearm lifts, letting me breathe.

"Hunter, wait," I gasp. "I'm not ready. You're going to—"

—*hurt me* is lost to a stunning slice of pain between my legs. I choke on a stuttered breath. Hunter turns my face away and mashes my cheek into the wall.

"Hunter, that hurts. You're hurting me."

He ignores my tattered sobs. I stuff my fist in my mouth to stopper the screams, in case the sound drives him into a frenzy. More of a frenzy.

Everything is agonising fire where he pistons into me. Acid and glass.

I bite my knuckle but the cut of teeth in my flesh is insignificant. I taste copper, bile, salt. I scrunch my eyes shut and pray to all the gods in all the universes for it to be over.

Hunter thrusts hard. Something snaps inside me. A scream breaks past the blockage of my fist. The shrieks hurt my own ears even though I'm the one making them. They echo in the room, my head, the corridor. They buzz in my teeth.

My world becomes a blinding flash of white. I realise I'm sitting on the floor, slumped against the wall. Hunter looms over me, wreathed in shadow. The only colour is the blood streaking his groin and pooling under my arse. He tucks his dick into his trousers, daubing his fingers red. Deft hands fasten his laces. Then he spins on his heel and leaves the room, the door sliding shut behind him.

An animal keening shivers from my ruined throat.

Is this the end Salam wanted? Me, in shock, bleeding and alone?

I tug on the material of my bodysuit, attempting to cover myself. The movement upsets my balance and I slide down the wall to flop on the floor, worsening the unholy conflagration in my lower body. Agony sparks on every shudder but I can't stop. I peel my bodysuit over clammy skin. My hands get tangled for several agonising minutes in the sleeves before I roll the material up my arms to my shoulders. The suit gapes at the chest.

Everything is slippery and red—my hands, the floor, the wall above me. Black feathers tease the edge of my vision. A spike of fear torments my heart rate but Hunter doesn't appear. The blackness creeps across my eyeballs, hazing all but the pain.

I jam my hand between the pallet and the bed slab without moving the rest of me. A hot line brands my cold yet sweaty palm. I wrap the knife in my fist and slide it clear. It's impossible to focus in the blurred black. More scorching lines trace my forearm when I slip the knife up my sleeve.

I want to secure it, keep it safe, but manual dexterity is beyond me. Breathing is also beyond me.

A shape leans over. A head and shoulders. Wings. Everything has fucking wings except me. Something tickles my chest.

Are they enjoying the sight of me exposed, shivering and covered in blood?

Darkness and pain smother the lick of anger.

"Please"—my voice breaks—"*don't.*"

And, just like Hunter, the figure ignores me.

21

I wake drowning in pink—the healing bath. I panic anyway and flail at the glass box. The lid refuses to budge under my clawing fingers.

"Calm yourself, child," comes Bronwyn's voice, muffled by the liquid in my ears and the roar of my pulse. "Then I will let you up. Too much is wasted otherwise."

I want to tell her where she can stick her waste but it was humanity's consumerism that got us into this mess. If we'd treated our planet and its resources as more than an all-you-can-eat buffet, I wouldn't be stuck in a tank of goo on the verge of a nervous breakdown.

I bang my fists against the glass and scream a bubble-less scream. My heart thunders too fast, too hard.

Or maybe not on the verge of a mental crisis so much as right in the middle of one.

The adrenaline evaporates to leave me hollow. I sag in the warm fluid and bump against the bottom. A headache sizzles between my temples and down my spine. My pelvis aches.

Anxiety skitters through my nerves. The glass lid disappears, distracting me. Bronwyn's gentle hands guide me, blinking, into the silvery light of the healing ward. I hug my knees to my chest. The hard line of the knife in my sleeve digs into my shin but I'm too numb to feel relief. Pink goop slops around me, and only then do I notice I'm shaking.

"You are a fragile human, child," Bronwyn says, patting my hair. "Why did you resist him?"

"I want him back. I want my angel back not the monster you've made." I lift my gaze, my eyes dry and burning. "I will save him, even if it breaks me."

There's a horrible grinding in my chest. It rips up my throat in place of sobs and tears.

Bronwyn cocks her head, her bony crest short and neat. "Why do you fight so? You could end your suffering. To die at one's own hand is honourable when one has committed a crime or become a burden."

"You think forcing me to kill myself is *honourable?*"

She tries to help me out of the bath but I bat her hands away. She tucks them to her chest, her head drawn back. My bare feet slap on the floor in a shower of droplets.

Whoops.

My bodysuit is as tattered as always, and sagging, but leached of blood and sweat. I tuck the knife arm across my stomach. Bronwyn's toenails are painted orange today.

She's the only Creator who shows any hint of colour or individuality. But I'm done guessing what it might mean.

I was so wrong before.

Bronwyn gestures to my usual slab at the edge of the hexagonal room. "Rest for a spell. You are still weak."

"Why are you healing me, making sure I *rest,* if you want me to die? That's the biggest goddamn waste of resources ever."

I stagger to the slab and hoist my arse onto the edge, refusing to lie down. I drum my heels against the side.

"I do not want you to die, child."

I swallow a hiccup. "You're the only one here who doesn't."

Bronwyn hooks a shiny stool from under the glass tank and perches on it, ruffling her wings. Her pale-grey skin complements her mauve bodysuit.

"Our empire is ancient," she says after a period of silence. "We have certain processes and rules we expect the younger civilisations to follow. Your universe has more portals to desolate planets than any other we have discovered so far. We have found no other sentient life except that on your home world. It is proof that humanity is savage. A rotten core."

"You sound just like Salam and Tallai." Bronwyn flinches but I keep talking. "How can you call us savage when you send your armies out to slaughter? You use torture and cruelty as a teachable moment."

"A firm hand ensures…" She shifts on the stool and stares at her toenails. "Compliance. To allow free rein would risk the stability of everything we have built."

I snort. "Your civilisation can't be that great if one tiny, far-away planet has the power to ruin it."

"There are factors in play you do not understand, child. Our province is but one cog of the empire. Our rule is strict because it must be. Failure to control the universes under our charge would be… shameful. To soften, to falter, would encourage rebellion."

"Rebellion is encouraged by oppression and injustice. Maybe it's time you judged yourselves instead of everyone else."

Bronwyn glances towards the doorway and lowers her voice. "Our weapons are all that stand between us and chaos."

"Or that's what they want you to think when, really, your weapons are all that maintain the tyranny," I say softly. "You keep them brutal and enslaved to their aggression so that you can stay in power."

Her navy and amethyst eyes meet mine. "Perhaps you do understand."

A blip of excitement stirs my pulse, sluggish after the last panic attack and healing session and thoughts of Hunter fracturing my pelvis.

I'm getting through to her. I have to be. Just like I'm getting through to Uziyah. Kind of. Hopefully.

I need their help. I need something to change or I'm not going to make it. I can't endure more of this.

"Let the angels choose a life for themselves. Let us go *home*," I whisper. "Help me, Bronwyn."

She clicks her beak. "Bronwyn?"

"Bronwyn'challi. Sorry. We humans like to abbreviate."

"You can call me Bronwyn. I do not mind it."

"You seemed affronted when I shortened Salam and Tallai's names."

"They are my elders. To say the full range of their names is a mark of respect."

"I'll say their full names when they deserve my respect." I quirk my mouth. "Which will be never."

Bronwyn chuckles, a slightly less grating cackle than Salam's or Tallai's. "Your civilisation is capricious. You speak when we would not dare."

"And is that because you respect them too much to offend or because you're afraid they'll sic their angels on you? Don't let creatures like Salam and Tallai rule out of fear." I pause for a breath, and some courage. "Will you help me?"

"I—"

"If you had let me carry you, we would have been here yesterday." Uziyah's disgruntled voice cuts off Bronwyn's response.

"You're not touching me, arsehole."

Steph clutches the doorway and staggers into the ward. Her face is pale and sweating, her eyes bright, but her jaw is set in a stubborn line.

"Steph! What are you doing here?"

She totters for me from one piece of equipment to the next. Bronwyn flutters to her feet when Steph grabs at the edge of the glass tank.

"You are in pain. Please, use my arm."

"What did she say?" Steph says.

I translate, and Steph takes the elongated limb without hesitation. Uziyah grits his teeth.

Steph plonks next to me on a relieved huff of breath. "Surly-chops said I could come get some magical healing or whatever."

Surly-chops—aka Uziyah—stomps to the stool vacated by Bronwyn and throws himself onto it. Metal shrieks in protest. He crosses his thick arms, his wings flicking his annoyance.

"I can still return you to your cell without the healing," he growls.

"I think you might be right about him," Steph says.

Uziyah's brow wrinkles. His pale eyes meet mine.

"Where's Greg?" I say instead of answering the question on his face.

"Back in the cell. Sir Scowls-A-Lot wouldn't let him come with." Steph turns to me, and gasps. "Maia! You look worse! What the hell happened? It's been two days—three? Greg counts. I can't be bothered."

She grips my chin and peers at my face. Worry clouds her eyes. Uziyah watches me in my periphery.

Because of course it was him who found me, broken and

bloody. Anyone else would have left me there. Or hurt me worse.

"They upped their game," I say, unable to stop the hitch in my voice.

Steph bares her teeth. "Those fuckers will pay for it."

Bronwyn bustles between us. Gestures and some explanation from me get Steph stretched out on the neighbouring slab, the translation liquid in her ears and the shroud covering her from chin to toes.

She grins. "Greg is going to lose his shit."

"Rest, now," Bronwyn says. "Let the healing shroud do its work."

How come Steph doesn't get called 'child'? I guess she is almost double my size. Tall and slim. Svelte—that's Steph. She also chose a great pair of tits for herself so that helps dispel the child thing.

I feel so much better having her with me. Best friends are a super power.

I glance at Uziyah. He's still frowning at me. Bronwyn regards him curiously then scoops a device off a shelf.

"Be still," she says, and places the device on his head.

It looks like a plain metal crown until the centre starts to glow violet. She perches a rectangular lens on the end of her beak. It flickers to show a tracery of black, like the branches of a tree.

Not a lens—a screen.

"What are you doing?" I say.

"Uziyah has been behaving oddly. I am scanning his cybernetics."

Uziyah's eyes widen. He schools his expression and narrows his gaze at me, as if it's my fault.

"Oddly how?" I say.

"He won his last two challenges but did not claim his victory." Bronwyn circles him, peering at the screen. "He has carried you to the healing ward twice of his own volition. He brought your other human because she was in pain."

"She is her best friend," Uziyah grumbles.

Steph raises her brow at me, and smirks. "Just how nice to him were you, Maia?"

I stick my tongue out. "Not as nice as I was to Hunter."

We share a fist bump while Uziyah's confused gaze ping-pongs between us.

"As I suspected," Bronwyn says, whipping the screen off her beak. "His cybernetics have been damaged."

Uziyah jolts, then flares his wings to stop himself from tumbling off the stool. Bronwyn plucks the scanner from his crown.

"I am damaged?" he says. "That is why I feel… different?"

I shake my head. "You're not damaged, Uziyah. This is how you behave without the cybernetics' interference."

He glowers. "I do not like it."

"There is an area in his brain where tissue has grown around the cybernetics, choking several branches. There is enough functioning technology to maintain his aggression, though it seems to be in balance with this more… compassionate side." Bronwyn gives him an appraising look.

Uziyah sneers. "I am not compassionate. I won my last two battles."

"Why didn't you take what you wanted?" I say softly.

A frown wrinkles his brow. He stares at his bare feet. His shoulders hunch.

"I did not… It did not… feel right. Not after…" He shakes

himself and glares at me. "Did you do this?"

I raise my hands. "I'd like to believe that treating you nice and being your friend is enough to change you, but this is on your society. When you were badly beaten—the second time—I think you got a brain injury. Would that be enough?"

We all look at Bronwyn. She rubs her beak.

"Brain injuries are uncommon. It is a level of brutality the Protectorate do not usually show each other. But, yes, if the healing tissue disrupted the integrity of the cybernetics, it would be enough."

"Holy shit," Steph breathes. Her awed gaze narrows at Bronwyn. "Are you going to take this news to those other two douchebags and have them fix it?"

"What are douchebags?" Bronwyn and Uziyah say together.

Steph smirks. "Those two specimens that stumbled out of *Jurassic Park*."

Bronwyn and Uziyah look no more enlightened. I turn a chuckle into a cough.

"Bronwyn has been keeping her true thoughts to herself for a long time, I think," I say, watching her carefully.

She bows her head. "I will leave Uziyah as he is. I will not tell the… douchebags."

A surprised laugh bursts from my chest, the sound absent so long, it seems alien. Steph joins in and we giggle until we're breathless, and my stomach hurts.

"Wait," I gasp, swiping at my watering eyes. "Uziyah—do you want to stay this way or do you want to go back to being a sneery, angry arsehole whose only joy is pummelling others in the arena? You get to choose this time."

He blinks at me. His gaze bounces to Steph and Bronwyn then back to me.

"I get to choose?"

"You get to choose." I swallow hard, the humour gone. "That's all Hunter ever wanted—a life he had chosen."

Uziyah's lip curls. "I do not like Hunter."

"You don't like the Creators' Hunter. My Hunter is a million times better than that bastard."

Uziyah scoffs but sits up straighter. "Fine. I will stay like this. I want to choose more things. I want to nap during the day and… read. I want to be able to read."

"You can do whatever you want. Without dominating or hurting anyone," I add quickly.

Steph slaps me on the shoulder. "You beautiful, bleeding-hearted romantic—you've done it again."

"What has she done?" Bronwyn says.

Steph grins and spreads her arms wide. "She's started another rebellion."

22

"What are you doing?"

Uziyah's voice jerks my gaze from the gleaming turquoise floor. I halt my hunched-shouldered shuffle instead of barrelling into him.

"I'm acting submissive," I say.

He tuts. "That will be a first."

He spins on his heel and continues his stomp down the corridor. His wings stretch, the tips brushing the pearly walls, then settle against his back. I trail after him, my eyes and face downcast. Each ache from my pelvis stirs a tickle of panic in my throat. I focus on my bare toes and the thud of Uziyah's gait instead of searching for a glimpse of black wings and laced boots and dark, dark eyes.

I hate that fear is the first thing I feel at the thought of seeing Hunter again.

The Creators will pay for that, too.

Uziyah weaves through the labyrinthine and unchanging corridors. I've been utterly lost since we left the healing ward. A door hisses open.

"What have you done to Steph, you angel prick?" Greg growls.

I slip around Uziyah's broad back. Greg stands with his fists clenched, glaring at the warrior, his hair tucked behind his ears.

"Steph's fine," I say. "We just came to get you."

Greg's eyes dart between me and Uziyah. "Jesus, you've tamed another one."

"I am not tame," Uziyah snarls.

Greg retreats, his hands raised. "Right. Course you're not."

"He's not tame but he is trying to be less of an arsehole," I say, giving Uziyah a pointed look.

He snorts and crosses his arms. "Perhaps I am *choosing* to be an arsehole."

Greg leans in, sparing the angel a wary glance.

"What's going on?" he whispers. "Have you found a way to get past the shit in their brains?"

"Not yet. But I've found us some allies."

Greg's eyes spark as brightly as his grin. "I knew you could do it, Angelfucker."

"Angel*tamer*," I say, my cheeks heating. "This time, we're not going to fuck the rest. We're going to free them."

Uziyah flicks his wings. "Come, feeble creature. Other human. We must not linger."

"Are you still going to keep calling me that?"

His grin mirrors Greg's. "You are feeble yet fierce. You have the endurance of a warrior, if not the stature."

Greg coughs a laugh. "He called you a short arse."

Grumbling, I follow Uziyah into the corridor. Greg's dress shoes scuttle to keep up. He shrugs his suit jacket on, smoothing the wrinkles from the sleeves. We walk in step behind Uziyah. My skin itches to be back in the healing ward where there's a modicum of safety.

"Where are you taking the humans, Uziyah?" a voice purrs

behind us.

Abayankari of the white, shining hair and perfect cheek-bones. Perfect tits, too. Her eyes are the same colour as the floor. Gleaming and malevolent. Her robe is loose and threaded with silver. She cocks a pale brow at Uziyah. Greg and I attempt to merge with the wall.

Uziyah sneers at her. "I am taking them to Salam'ack'tai'mo ran."

"I am surprised you still have his attention."

"Jealous, 'Kari?"

"*Abayankari*," she growls.

"What are they saying?"

I jump at Greg's murmur in my ear.

"Just the usual posturing," I say out the side of my mouth. "My dick's bigger than your dick et cetera."

Abayankari's sea-green gaze rakes over me. Her lip curls to match Uziyah's.

"Hunter has been too gentle with you, human." Her sneer slides into a wicked little smile that chills me to my toes. "I will not be so lenient. He has permitted me to continue your suffering." She lifts her focus to Uziyah. "Bring her to the arena when the Creators are done with her."

"You do not command me, 'Kari," Uziyah says.

She crowds the bulkier angel, though he stands his ground. She's an inch taller, but slimmer. Long, athletic muscles. Her white wings curl around them both and stir their hair.

"When I am done with the human, I will take you next." She bends closer, her lips at his ear. "And it will not be like we battled before. You will not enjoy it."

She whips around, the sweep of her wings shunting him back a step. He gives a tiny shudder but freezes when he catches me watching him. Abayankari looms over me. Greg puffs out his chest but she doesn't spare him a glance.

"I will cut you until you yield," she says in the same soft, evil purr. "When you are slippery and defeated, you will please me with your mouth or I will slide my knife between your legs and climax to your screams."

My thighs press together. Abayankari leaps into flight while I'm deciding whether to faint or vomit. She swoops around a corner, leaving us blessedly alone in the corridor.

"What did she say? It didn't sound good, whatever it was." Greg touches my arm. "You okay, Maia?"

I manage a nod, though my whole body feels cold and bloodless.

"We won't let that psycho touch you. Right, Uziyah?"

Uziyah inclines his head. "I will distract her if I must."

"You like her."

Uziyah's lips thin at Greg's statement. "I respected her. Our fights were legendary. But now she is… intense."

"I hate to break it to you, man, but you're all like that."

We hustle along. I can't help glancing over my shoulder.

"Whatever we're doing, it has to happen today. I can't…" I meet Uziyah's eyes. The understanding in them nearly undoes me. "I just can't," I finish on a strangled whisper.

"She will not touch you," Uziyah says softly.

Greg squeezes my arm again. "We won't let them hurt you anymore."

We reach the healing ward without any other warriors threatening rape and mutilation. The door glides shut behind us. Bronwyn taps on a rectangle of wall next to it, and a lock clunks.

"Look, Maia!"

Steph grins at me and skips around the room, kicking her legs high. She throws her arms around Greg, attempting to pick him up.

She staggers. "Christ, you're heavier than you look, prickles."

"What is it with you and that big blue bastard?" he huffs. "I'm not prickly."

"That sounded prickly to me."

Steph plants a smacker of a kiss on his cheek then dances across to me and twirls me around. I shove the fear down deep, and laugh at her antics. Greg looks dazed while his fingers stroke his cheek.

Bronwyn folds her hands. "Your human—"

"Steph," Steph supplies helpfully, spinning me into a tango.

"—Steph," Bronwyn continues, "has an imbalance in her brain that cannot be healed. That imbalance also allows her body to attack itself. Her pain will return but she will be comfortable for now."

"Thank you, Bronwyn," I say.

Steph dips me. "Even they can't cure fibromyalgia and rheumatoid arthritis despite their fancy-pants technology. Bit of a downer but it feels amazing to be able to move."

"Probably just as well. If you were healed, I'd be the glamorous assistant and you'd be the one taking over the world."

"Nah. Too much work."

Uziyah leans his hip on a slab. "You humans are strange."

"Okay, if I don't get some of this translation stuff, I'm going to get mad," Greg says.

Steph smirks. "See—prickly."

Steph and I perch shoulder to hip on a raised pallet. Bronwyn guides Greg onto his own slab and squirts the goop in his ears.

He shakes his head, opening his jaw wide and jerking it side to side like a startled cow still trying to chew the cud.

"It fizzes," he yells.

"Greg, this is Bronwyn," I say. "Bronwyn—Greg."

She dips her beak. "Pleased to meet you, loud human."

"Holy shit! I can hear both the translated and untranslated language. This is amazing!" Greg bounces on the slab. "Can it understand any language?"

"Any known language in the universes."

"What if it comes across a new language?"

"Then it will require a period of learning and adjustment but it will decipher it given enough data."

"How long would—"

"Greg," Steph says, rolling her eyes, "this is not the time for you to geek out."

Greg ducks his head. "Right, sorry."

Steph aims her smirk at me. "What's the plan, boss?"

I shift on the slab under the weight of everyone's attention, and stroke the knife in my sleeve for reassurance.

"Well…" I clear my throat. "Who wants to commandeer a spaceship?"

"This is the best day ever," Greg sighs.

23

"We need to get the angels away from here—away from the Creators. No offence, Bronwyn."

I lean forward, my elbows on my knees, chin planted on my fists. Steph, Greg, Bronwyn and Uziyah complete our pow wow in the healing ward.

"But what about the stuff in their heads?" Steph says, her hip pressed to mine, heels kicking against the slab. "The Creators can boss them around from a distance."

Uziyah shifts on the tiny stool, perched next to Bronwyn. "They cannot command across universes. They must be within range of the planet where we are stationed."

"How close were they when they called the retreat from Earth?" I say.

"The shuttle was orbiting Jupiter."

"Still pretty fucking far," Steph mutters. "But that point is moot since the angels are not exactly going to come quietly, are they?"

I raise my gaze to Bronwyn. Her navy and amethyst eyes flick between us. Her wings quiver.

"They may be your tools but the Protectorate are dangerous," I say slowly. "Surely you have a way to control them beyond the cybernetics?"

Bronwyn taps a finger against her throat. "We are planners. Creators. We have many contingencies for all foreseeable outcomes."

"Great," Greg mutters, sitting cross-legged on the floor. "Let's hope one of those foreseeables isn't a hostile takeover by a bunch of humans."

I wave an encouraging hand at Bronwyn. Her beak is rigid but a smile sparkles in her eyes.

"So, yes, child—we have the means of mass control." She slides a glance at Uziyah. "All our ships are fitted with a mechanism for the dispersion of sedative gas."

Uziyah wrinkles his nose. "It smells like the excretions of an oolingdan."

Greg, naturally, perks up. "What's that?"

"An invertebrate creature not unlike your slugs but fifty times larger. They are found in the Narthrax system."

Greg hugs his knees, his face alight. "And are they—"

Steph prods her toe into his ribs. "Rein it in, prickles. We're on the clock."

"Just you wait," he huffs, swatting at her foot. "I'm going to come up with a nickname you'll *hate*."

"Surprised you haven't done it already."

"Nothing that can be said out loud," he says, and she rewards him with another toe poke.

While Greg is squirming, I refocus on Bronwyn. "So we can knock out all the angels. What about the Creators?"

"The gas will render them unconscious but their command hubs will issue a warning when the mechanism is triggered."

"Command hubs?"

"The devices Salam'ack—" Bronwyn clears her throat as if she has a hairball. "The devices Salam and Tallai wear on their wrists."

I grin at her. "I knew you were a rebel the second I saw your toenails."

She wiggles her painted toes. "They will don their respirators as soon as they receive the alert. They are unlikely to be caught unawares."

"So we have to catch them first."

"I can overpower them," Uziyah says. "They will not expect it."

Bronwyn pads to a silver cabinet on the far side of the room. Metal rattles. She returns and uncurls her long fingers to show us four objects balanced on her palm, each with two mesh plugs connected by a loop of tubing containing a blue liquid.

"You must put these in your nostrils or you will succumb to the sedative."

I pluck one between my fingers. "What if some of us aren't near Salam or Tallai to hear the alarm? We might have to split up to pull this off."

"If you smell an oolingdan then you will know."

"And what does an oolong smell like?"

"Bad," Uziyah says over Greg's muffled snort.

We tuck the respirators into our various sleeves and pockets.

"What if we breathe through our mouths?" Greg says.

Bronwyn cocks her head. "You breathe through your mouth?"

"Don't breathe through your mouth," Greg sighs. "Got it."

Steph taps my knee until I look at her. "But we should stick together, right? If we can?"

"Yeah—stick together. Where can we trigger the gas?" I say to Bronwyn.

"All the ship's controls are accessed from the room where I first met you," she says.

The silver dome with the screens. Of course. No idea how to get there.

"Okay. So we gas the ship and fly it back to Earth." I scrub my face. "God, this is crazy. Storming a castle is one thing but how are we supposed to navigate a bloody spaceship across universes?"

Steph squeezes my knee. "We stopped the *apocalypse*. We can do this for the ones we love plus the rest of our friends. And maybe we'll get new friends if the other angels aren't still a bunch of arseholes when we get that crud out of their heads."

"Speaking of crud." I tilt my face towards Bronwyn. "Do you have anything on this technological marvel of a ship to remove the cybernetics?"

"Alas, we do not, child. We have no need to remove our means of control, only the drive to enhance it."

Anxiety threatens to overwhelm me. How are we going to destroy the cybernetics without hurting the angels? This is all for nothing if I can't get Hunter back. I want Hunter back. I can't deal with the monster he's become.

I bat at the air as if I can shoo the panic away. "We figure that out later. Can we at least keep everyone asleep for a while? Are there pods on this thing—those tubes with the squidgy pink goo?"

"There are stasis capsules, yes," Bronwyn says, her hands folded in her lap.

"Okay," I say. I say it again until I'm a little calmer. Only five or six times. "We restrain Salam and Tallai then go to the control room together. Trigger the gas. Put the angels on ice. Get Salam or Tallai to guide the ship home. I wouldn't mind handing them over to the government to poke and prod and experiment on."

Steph jiggles beside me. "As long as I can kick them in the nuts for all the harm they've caused."

"If they even have nuts," Greg says.

"Testicles," Uziyah provides in response to Bronwyn's furrowed brow.

I slide off the slab and shake the nervous energy from my limbs, though it buzzes in my fingers and toes. The iron knife slips down my sleeve. I adjust its position, making sure the respirator is still in place. Steph follows my movements.

"You managed to steal it back off him?"

I nod. "It wasn't easy."

An understatement for the most harrowing and painful experience of my life.

I meet Uziyah's gaze. Shame and embarrassment burn my cheeks.

"What did you steal?" he says.

"A weapon. But I won't use it unless I have to."

"You smuggled a weapon onto the shuttle?" His ashy eyes sweep me from head to toe. I wait for his sneer but a smirk ticks his mouth upward. "You are crafty, feeble creature. Very crafty."

Steph bristles. "She's not—"

I wrap my fingers around her bicep before she launches at Uziyah to defend my honour.

"Don't," I say. "For him, it's a term of endearment."

His smirk widens to a grin. "We are friends now."

She grumbles but subsides. I take a deep breath. And another. Time to rally the troops with an order to move out, since I'm the bloody leader of the resistance *again*. I open my mouth.

A fist thunders on the door to the healing ward.

"Bronwyn'challi, why is this door locked? Open it at once."

Bronwyn hustles to the entrance, her wings fluttering in agitation. "Apologies, Tallai'sig'chai. I have been having trouble with the locking mechanism. A moment while I disable it."

Steph hops from foot to foot. Greg looks like he might bolt. Uziyah glowers at the doorway as if it's offended him.

"What do we do, boss?" Steph hisses. "Hide? Pounce? Pretend we're sleeping?"

I straighten to my full height, which barely puts me at Steph's breastbone. My pulse thuds in the hollow of my throat.

"We fight," I say.

"What if he's not alone?"

I eye the warrior angel hulking over all of us. A pang strums through my chest.

"Neither are we," I say softly.

Tallai sweeps into the healing ward with an imperious sniff. The door glides shut behind him. He brands us all with his bright, fluorescent gaze.

"What are the other humans doing here?"

Bronwyn bobs her head at him, her chest curling even further inwards. "Uziyah reported in passing that one of the humans was experiencing pain. I asked him to bring them both to the ward so that I might examine them. I admit a certain… curiosity for their species."

"Curiosity, Bronwyn'challi? Or has your youthful innocence been sullied by their proximity?" Tallai narrows his eyes. "And Uziyah. Abayankari told us your tale of taking the humans to Salam'ack'tai'moran, yet he made no such request. To find you here of your own volition amongst insurgents is most disturbing."

Unease ripples through my gut.

Have we been discovered already? Is Salam in the corridor with a mob of angels to make us regret our defiance? Is Hunter waiting to drag me away for more torture?

Uziyah bows low, his feathers brushing the floor. "I lied to Abayankari. I did not want her to know where I was going."

"And why is that?"

Tallai stalks deeper into the room. He spreads his dark wings wide, the sheen of purple gleaming under the lights. I inch further from Steph and Greg, giving myself room to manoeuvre.

"She would have taken the female from me." Uziyah lifts only his face, his body still bent in supplication. "But I wanted to be the one to break her."

"You seem to have grown close to the human." Tallai clucks his tongue. "Some might even say sympathetic."

A cruel smirk tilts Uziyah's lips. He straightens with an expression of perfect arrogance.

"Humans are easy to fool, Creator," he says. "The feeble creature believes I am her ally. I was going to use that trust to shatter her spirit."

My mouth drops open. Steph makes a strangled noise in her throat that sounds like, "You back-stabbing son of a cockroach." Greg frowns between Uziyah and Tallai.

Is Uziyah acting to throw Tallai off? Or has he manipulated me exactly where he wants me?

Tallai chuckles. "Yes, the faith of humanity is quite pitiful. I regret, then, that I spoiled your ploy."

Uziyah dips his head. "Permit me to end her punishment and all is forgiven, Creator."

"Hunter and Abayankari await her presence in the arena. If she survives their special challenge, you have my permission. Salam'ack'tai'moran and I are eager to witness."

Fear crackles down my spine.

Tallai flicks his long fingers. "Bring her."

Another eager bow. "And the others?"

"Bronwyn'challi will return them to their cell. If they are any trouble, they can join their rebel leader in the arena. Their species has wasted enough of our resources and attention. It has been an embarrassment for our province, and a hard lesson."

Firm fingers manacle my bicep. My wobbling legs threaten to pitch me to my knees at Uziyah's feet.

This can't be happening. We were about to resist. *To win.*

Steph growls and leaps for Uziyah. A slap of his wing sends her reeling into Greg, and they tumble to the ground in a cursing jumble of limbs. Bronwyn wrings her hands at the edge of the room. Uziyah tows me over to the gloating Creator.

"What did we tell you about defiance, idiot human?" Tallai's dry, grey tongue licks across his bared teeth. "While you perish in the arena, Devinon will mark their flesh for your scheming. They will return to their world, but it will not be whole."

He moves to spin on his heel. The grip on my bicep disappears, leaving tingles in its wake. Uziyah places a reverent hand on the Creator's thin shoulder.

Tallai cocks his head. "What are you—"

Uziyah ploughs his fist into Tallai's gut. Tallai's whoosh of breath blasts his reptilian scent into my face. He folds at his freakish stork legs. Uziyah swings another punch but Tallai snaps upright, slamming his bony crest into the angel's chin. Uziyah thumps on his arse beside the disentangling Steph and Greg, his eyes dazed.

"Traitorous creature," Tallai hisses.

He swipes a long finger across the hub on his wrist. Uziyah's spine arches, the rest of him rigid and quivering. A pained bark escapes the clamp of his teeth. His thrashing wings catapult one of the metal stools into my legs, bruising my shin.

Tallai taps his device. "You will all suffer for this."

Slimmer, lighter fingers wrap around his wrist and yank the

contraption from his arm. Tallai backhands Bronwyn before she can retreat with her prize, the slap of flesh echoing in the domed space. She crumples at the base of a slab. The hub skitters under the tank of pink glop. Tallai crouches low, reaching for it, his wings hunched and shivering in fury.

"How can one human have such influence?" he mutters to himself. "One snivelling, pathetic—"

I hammer the seat of the stool into the back of his head where bony crest ends and bald flesh begins. The metal makes a satisfying *thonk* against his thick skull. Tallai sprawls on his face, his beak gouging a divot in the floor. His shoulder nudges the tank, and pink liquid swirls, contained by the lid. His wings flop flat and still.

The stool clangs at my feet.

"Bloody hell, Uziyah," I gasp. "Give us a signal next time."

A groan is the only response from the angel, his arm flung across his face. Steph and Greg coax him to his feet. Steph pats at imaginary dust then seems to realise she's stroking Uziyah's bare torso. She tucks her hands under her armpits.

"Sorry about the cockroach thing," she says.

He grunts and massages his jaw. I hurry to Bronwyn's side. She props herself up, her fingers brushing the dark bloom on her pale cheek.

"I have never been struck before," she says softly.

"Neither had I until this place."

She hesitates but takes my hand and I pull her upright. She wobbles, bracing her palm on the slab. A shudder rustles her pastel-coloured wings then she straightens to her full height.

"We must bind and gag Tallai so he cannot call for help," she says.

"I have just the thing." Greg shucks his dress shoe, scuffed beyond repair, and peels off his black sock, wiggling his blunt toes. His grin is malicious. "Shame for him I haven't been in the windy cleaning tube today."

Uziyah drags the unconscious Creator from under the healing tank and pries his beak open. Greg stuffs his sock in Tallai's gullet, grimacing when his hand scrapes against the leathery tongue. Bronwyn loops a strip of bandage around to fix the garment in place, tying the material at the back of Tallai's skull. Another loop holds his beak shut. More bandages secure his wrists, wings and ankles until he's wrapped in a silken cocoon, like a spider's next meal.

I scoop the command hub from the floor and turn it over in my fingers. Strange symbols cover the screen, occasionally shimmering. I hold it away from me so I don't trigger anything.

Uziyah would not be amused by an accidental shocking.

Steph peers at the device over my shoulder. "Can we use it to gas the ship from here?"

I hand the alien thing to Bronwyn. She prods at the screen, her brow knitted.

"It requires a master code," she says, giving it back to me. "The higher-level commands will not function without it."

"So we storm the castle." Steph cracks her knuckles. "At least this time, I can contribute."

I cradle the device. A sick throb pulses in my gut and behind my eyes.

"They're waiting for us." My voice cracks. "If we don't go…"

"They will come looking," Uziyah finishes, his words solemn.

I raise my gaze to his. "We have to go to the arena to neutralise Salam."

He nods. Greg pales.

"But that white-haired psycho… Abayankari…"

"We don't have a choice. Uziyah and I will keep them occupied. You three gas the ship." I slide the hub onto my wrist to distract myself from the hard knot in my throat. "We'll have to synchronise our attacks. How much time do you need?"

Bronwyn taps the screen. Two symbols flicker in the top-left corner. The first looks like a triangle that's fractured at the core.

"When the second unit is the same, I will trigger the gas," she says.

"So we take Salam out quietly before that. How long is it?"

Bronwyn wrinkles her brow. "I do not know in human terms."

"Thirty minutes," Uziyah says.

Thirty minutes! I swallow hard. How am I going to survive thirty minutes in the arena with Hunter, never mind Abayankari? Uziyah can only do so much.

"Won't Salam be suspicious if you show up and the other dinosaur's not with you?" Steph says.

"Maybe but…"

She huffs. "We don't have a choice."

She pulls me into a hug. Firm arms circle me from behind. A reminder of when they both comforted me in their cell. The burning, grinding panic in my chest is the same.

"Be careful, Maia," Steph says into my hair. "Stall as much as you can."

"Stay out of reach of that white-haired bitch." Greg clears his throat. "And, uh… Hunter, too."

My laugh is bitter. "I don't think I'll have a choice in that, either."

"Hold out until you can get to Salam and they succumb to the gas." Steph gives me a squeeze. "We won't let you down."

"Hurry," I whisper. "Just *hurry*."

25

Uziyah drops us straight to the floor of the arena past tiers and tiers of silent, watchful angels. The space is packed, the air thick with the anticipation of violence. Uziyah's knees bend to absorb the impact of our landing. My stomach sinks past the band of his arm and settles somewhere around my toes.

He offered to hold me against his chest but I couldn't do it. Hunter held me like that. Cradled in his arms. Warm and safe in the curve of his body. I'd rather be carried like a sack of potatoes than reminded of what I've lost.

Though another reminder sneers at me from across the oval space. Malice glitters in Hunter's dark eyes, heightened by the fall of his hair. It's like staring into the soul of a wild animal through the bars of its cage. Except Hunter has no soul.

Abayankari stands at his side. Their wings graze, black against white. She's changed her outfit from when we met her in the corridor to a black leather bodice and skirt, slit to the thigh.

The perfect match for Hunter.

Salam parts the ferns over the banister in the lowest observation booth. "Where is Tallai'sig'chai?"

I get my feet under me and Uziyah steps away, his focus on the Creator. I smooth my sleeves down, making sure the knife and the command hub remain hidden.

"He is returning the other two rebels to their cell," Uziyah says. "The healer was examining them."

Salam clicks his tongue. "We will wait for him, though I am loath to delay. I grow tired of the resilience of humans."

My fingers itch to swipe the command hub and check the symbols. Neutralising Salam is going to be difficult with our audience, though at least Bronwyn, Steph and Greg don't have to wade through a ship of angels. Most of them are here, eager to watch my final battle.

I pray it doesn't turn out to be the battle they're anticipating.

Sweat slicks the cleft of my spine and pools at my lower back, sticking the material of the bodysuit to my skin. My palms are hot and damp, though the rest of me is cold to the bone.

"Let us play with her while we wait," Hunter says. "Let us play with them both."

Crap. *Crapcrapcrap*. It's too soon.

Salam gives an imperious nod. "I will allow it for Uziyah's dishonesty. The human's continued influence. Maim but do not destroy. Not yet."

Muscles bunch. Feral grins flash. Uziyah widens his stance into a crouch, his arms spread and ready to grapple. My heart thuds, sick and exhausted.

I can't fight him again. I'm not built for war. All I can do is stall.

"I'll forgive you, Hunter." My words rush out. "When you return to yourself. None of this is your fault."

Hunter halts Abayankari's leap with an arm across her ample chest. Impatience bristles her feathers but she subsides, scowling at me and licking her teeth.

Hunter smirks. "The creature I was is gone. He was an

embarrassment to his race. A warrior is not *gentle*. I would rather die than be him again."

I clench my left fist. Our wedding rings bite into my flesh.

"He was a better man than you'll ever be."

"Because I am not a man. They are not my equal. *You* are not my equal. Dominating you was not worth the wait. Your mewls were as pathetic as Uziyah's."

His cruel smile slices deep. Humiliation and shame burn in my cheeks.

Uziyah curls his fingers. "And yet here she stands. Unbroken, despite your worst."

"That was not my worst." Hunter's mouth twists. "Are you coupling her now, Uziyah? Is she the only creature you can dominate?"

He sounds exactly like one of the sadistic angels we fought during the apocalypse.

Amusement shivers through the spectating warriors. Salam frowns from his lofty perch.

"Riot," he hisses, and the brown-haired male shoves forward a few levels up, "find Tallai'sig'chai and see what delays him. He is unresponsive to my missives."

That'll be why the hub keeps vibrating on my wrist.

"Yes, Creator."

The angel leaps over the balcony, zooms across the arena and swoops above the heads of his brethren in the opposite tier, disappearing beyond the archway in the back. Salam returns his focus to us, regarding our exchange with greedy interest.

How much time has passed? I press my arm to my thigh and coax my sleeve higher with my pinkie to expose the screen of the command hub. Still only one, fractured triangle. Each interminable second drags a sharpened claw across my sanity.

If we go for Salam too soon, we'll be mangled beneath the fists of his furious warriors. If we wait too long, he'll be alerted by the gas. And we'll still get mangled. Will Riot check the healing ward first and find the trussed Tallai? Will he report back and ruin our plans?

"I do not couple with humans," Uziyah growls as if we weren't interrupted, "but anyone who challenges you is a friend of mine."

Hunter scoffs. "Your *friend* is about to be weeping meat beneath Abayankari's blade."

"How quickly you ally with someone you called weak, 'Kari—Abayankari," Uziyah says, his tone matching Hunter's despite the slight hitch. "Yet we have both lost to his challenge."

"But she did not whimper and whine when I claimed my victory," Hunter sneers.

Abayankari preens and curls against his side. "The new Hunter showed me what I have been lacking. He is no longer a lesser male." Her disdainful gaze adds the unspoken *unlike you*.

Her hand skims across Hunter's chest to dip into the laced neck of his black shirt and stroke his pec. She grinds against his hip and hooks one long leg around his waist, the material of her skirt parting to show a shapely calf and creamy skin. Her hair is a waterfall of white, shimmering around her wings.

Anger crackles between my clenched teeth. The heat of it evaporates my fear and anxiety.

"Stop. Touching. Him," I snarl. "He's not yours."

She laughs, and it's as perfect as her face. "Insolent human. For that, I will cut out your tongue. Then you will rut on my blade as if it is the cock you crave."

She dives for me, brutal glee brightening her face. I yelp.

25

Can't help it. Uziyah jumps to intercept but a streak of black collides with him and throws him into the wall.

Then I can't focus on them anymore.

A dagger appears in Abayankari's hand—not a soulreaver, thank goodness. It slashes for me in an arc. I pull my iron knife and throw myself from her path, my shoulder slamming the floor and sending a rattle through my teeth. Wind stirs my hair. I scramble to my feet. Abayankari pirouettes in mid-air, touching down with the grace of a ballerina. Male grunts provide our backdrop. She opens her mouth, no doubt to gloat or mock or threaten—probably all three—and I sprint for her. Her eyes widen. I catch the wrist of her knife hand. She blocks my stab for her throat, her fingers branding my forearm. Our harsh breaths fill the frozen moment, our arms clasped wide. She smells like roses. Her arching wings loom over me. She is taller, prettier, *worthier,* than I am.

I ram my knee between her legs.

Maybe the psycho will stop fixating on that part of my anatomy for a minute.

Her startled huff brushes my upturned face. Her grip loosens. I punch my knife between her ribs. She staggers back but I follow.

No mercy—that's something she understands.

My blade slips to the hilt in her gut. Silver and yellow froth stain her leather bodice. The back of her hand cracks across my jaw, spinning me around. I lose my grip on my knife, and reality. There's only the taste of blood in my mouth.

The device on my wrist emits a shrill whoop, deafening in the hush of the arena. An echo drifts from the tiers above.

I'm lying on the floor, my cheek pressed to spongy material that smells like rust and burning plastic. I shove onto my hands and knees. The world tilts, see-saws, then steadies. My jaw aches. The device on my wrist shows two fractured triangles.

Shit.

"What human trickery is this?" Salam roars. "Why do you have a command hub? *Where is Tallai'sig'chai?*"

Abayankari kneels a few feet away, staring at her hands covered in sickly bubbles and silver. Fascinated by her own blood, like Hunter was when I stabbed him with an iron sword. Hunter pummels Uziyah against the wall, the constant *whack-whack-whack* of his fists making my stomach clench. Uziyah sags, his eyes half-lidded. Barely conscious. Loose feathers flutter at his feet, ripped out in clumps.

I whip the respirator from my sleeve and shove the plugs deep in my nostrils. The air holds a hint of spoiled meat and sewage. I run at Hunter and throw myself onto his back between his wings. One arm wraps around his throat while I grab at his cheek with the other, twisting his head away from Uziyah. I tuck my face into the back of his neck and grip his ribs with my thighs.

His scent of ice, the familiar solidness of him, assaults me with a confusing mix of longing, grief and terror. The ghost of every wound he's dealt me throbs in sync.

He claws at my arm around his throat, and I scream into his nape. A fist bunches in my hair, tugging hard. I try to resist but my grip loosens at the shrieking agony in my scalp. Hunter drags me over his shoulder by the hair and launches me into Uziyah. We crumple to the floor.

Hunter is all savage eyes and high cheekbones as he stares down at us. A wad of my hair flutters in his hand.

"Where are you going?" Salam shrieks. "Kill the human!"

Angels pause in the tiers, their backs turned as they filter for the exits. Confusion passes like whispers through the crowd.

"The scent…" Markian says hesitantly. "It means we go to the stasis pods."

How well-trained they are.

"It will be cancelled momentarily," Salam hisses. "Rend the human limb from limb."

Every warrior angel in the arena takes flight.

And dives for me.

26

Hunter's slim and beautiful fingers wrap around my throat. He slams me against the wall in the same spot he was battering Uziyah.

My ribs won't last as long beneath the onslaught of his fists.

Shadows darken the sky as wings fill my vision, obscuring my glimpse of stars and oblivion through the window in the roof. The rustle and flap of thousands of angels is deafening. Hunter arches his black feathers, caging me against the wall and holding the other warriors at bay.

"Uziyah," I choke. "Respirator."

The clamp of Hunter's hand prevents me from angling my head to see Uziyah at our feet. It also stops me breathing through my mouth and inhaling the gas by accident. Stops me breathing at all, in fact.

But if we don't neutralise Salam, we're screwed. He'll soon realise, after a few swipes of his elongated finger, that the system keeps reactivating as soon as he cancels it. One command from him to send angels to the control room and this rebellion will crumble quicker than a person shot with an arrow.

"Did you think you could master *my* ship? *My* weapons?" Salam says from somewhere in the melee. Somewhere close.

"Your last moments will be steeped in pain for your disobedience. Make her suffer, Hunter. Make her regret."

"With pleasure," Hunter purrs.

His lips stretch in a smile. If I had any breath left to give, I would have lost it.

His hand loosens. I suck air through my nostrils, fighting against the drag of the filtered plugs. The lack of oxygen and the effort to inhale send dizziness fizzing in my skull.

Hunter leans close, and his mouth brushes my ear. Gentle—a lover's caress. Fear and panic twist my gut.

Salam glares at me over Hunter's shoulder before returning his focus to his command hub and stabbing at the screen. Fans hum in the walls. A maelstrom of angels surrounds Salam but they don't advance. They hover and wait and watch.

"Uziyah!" I squeak.

I asked Bronwyn how long the gas took to have an effect. Uziyah translated her answer to mean three minutes. It'll be longer while Salam and Bronwyn wrestle for control. But what if Uziyah is too weak to help before Salam commands his army to descend on the control room?

Then I will be very messily, horribly dead in the next few seconds.

"Do not call for him, pathetic creature," Hunter whispers silkily. "Is it not me you love?"

The original word in the angel's language—*criensalla*—ghosts beneath the translation.

Hunter places his palm on my chest, the touch light and tender. Salam growls but my husband ignores it. He raises his midnight-blue gaze to mine. Cruelty swims in the depths of his pupils. My command hub bleats but the sound is distant and muffled beneath the rushing in my ears.

"That means your heart belongs to me," he says in the same sultry tone, his eyes dark and alien. "So I intend to take it."

He curls his fingers on my chest. His nails catch in the material of my bodysuit. They press into my skin, bruising flesh against bone.

"Don't Hunter," I yelp. "Please."

Another alarm from the device on my wrist. No more hum of fan-assisted ventilation from the walls.

"Who else have you recruited to aid you?" Salam hisses. "How many of my Protectorate have you polluted with your humanity? No matter. *Finish it,* Hunter, then we will finish them."

Salam really is as arrogant as his creations. He thinks he has all the power here.

I hope he's wrong.

Feathers tickle my leg. Hunter grunts. His hold on my throat and chest relaxes further. He bends his head and swipes at something. Uziyah rolls into view, dodging Hunter's fist. Instead of attacking again, he leaps for Salam beneath the bobbing feet of thousands of hovering angels.

Salam snaps his beak, a respirator buried in his nostrils. He swipes the screen of his hub. Uziyah crashes to the floor in a quivering heap and clutches his head.

"Arsehole," he manages to sneer, though it ends in a whimper. Blue-liquid-filled tubing loops under his nose.

Pride at his defiance heats my chest and melts my frozen muscles. Hunter's attention has been pulled to Salam and the rebelling Uziyah, the rest of the Protectorate also observing the spectacle.

"Sorry, Hunter," I say.

Hunter's head whips around. His nails gouge my chest

through the slash his sword left in my bodysuit. I kick him between the legs.

I'm doing that a lot today.

He staggers back and sits hard on his arse, blinking up at me. Abayankari crawls for us with murder in her eyes and a trail of bloody froth behind her. I skip around them both and run for Salam. Indignation bristles in a million feathers. Angels swoop for me. They barge shoulders, fighting each other to reach me. Fingers catch my hair. I launch myself at Salam and tackle him around his bent-back knees. His hunched body folds over me, his wings slapping and smothering. He smells strangely sweet, like burnt marshmallows.

"Destroy her!" he roars, the force of his words vibrating his frame of leather and bones.

I scramble away from the frantic flap of his wings. My heart jams my throat, expecting clawing hands and choking feathers and agony.

But there's something wrong with the angels.

Figures dip in the vastness of the arena. Wings flare without rhythm. A frown mars every perfect face. Markian drops to his feet, stumbles, then falls to his knees, his red wings quivering. Another joins him. Another. And another. Bodies smack into each other, forming piles. Limp carcasses tumble to the base until there's not a patch of floor free except around me, Salam and Uziyah.

A hand grabs my ankle.

Hunter drags himself closer, his teeth gritted. His eyes are hooded and unfocused. Abayankari is the bottom layer of a tower of arms and legs and wings. My knife gleams dully through the spill of her white hair.

Salam straightens to his full height, brushing at his bodysuit and regarding me snootily down the length of his beak. The loop of the respirator curves over the top.

Uziyah writhes on the ground.

Hunter's fingers tighten on my ankle. Bones grind together.

"I will destroy you," he growls, though the words are slurred.

I yank my leg. Slackening fingers flop from my ankle and squeeze at nothing but air. I crouch next to him, my fingertip tracing his sharp cheekbone, his head pillowed on his outstretched arm.

"No, you won't," I say softly. "But I'll destroy you."

His muscles go lax and his eyes slip shut. Velvet wings sprawl to either side.

I execute a roll not quite as effective as Uziyah's, softened yet awkward by the angel carpet now covering the floor. My hand closes on the iron knife. I stand and face Salam across the unconscious Hunter, mountains of comatose Protectorate piled high all around us.

I hope the angels near the bottom don't suffocate.

"What are you going to do now, Salam?" I say. "Seems I'm the only one with a weapon."

He bares his pointy teeth. "As if you could stop me, human. You have simply delayed your fate, not altered it."

His wings snap out. The muscles in his legs bunch.

I'm too far to reach him.

Broad fingers grab his ankle. The fresh bruises on mine pulse in sympathy. Salam squawks as Uziyah yanks him back down. The Creator trips on Uziyah's prone form, landing on his back, his legs in the air. Uziyah's face is pale and lined with pain.

This will be the last time the Creators hurt any of my angels.

I climb across the bodies and rip the command hub from

Salam's wrist.

27

I now have two command hubs on my right wrist. I'm starting to feel like a gangster with all the bling, and a knife up my sleeve. Not so much the saggy bodysuit held together by threads, one sharp tug from disintegrating. I still have my wedding underwear on. The tulle and golden leaves have lost their lustre somewhat.

This was not the honeymoon Hunter and I planned.

I twist my head, my body tucked under Uziyah's arm. His wings beat hard. Salam curses and wriggles in Uziyah's grip, his arms pinned by the angel. A sprawled, black-winged, black-clothed figure dwindles on the floor below us, surrounded by a sea of white and gold and jewel colours. Unmoving and alone.

I force my eyes away.

Uziyah swoops over the lowest balcony, stirring the ferns. He places me on my feet. Salam tumbles arse over crest with another indignant squawk.

"Traitor," he hisses. "Shameful, ungrateful *traitor*. We gave you *life*. We *own* you."

Uziyah plants his hands on his hips and glares down at the Creator. "Now that you cannot melt my brain to keep me compliant, what exactly are you going to do about it?"

178

Salam's beak snaps but no words come out.

"You will pay for this," he finally says.

He gathers his legs under him and rises to his feet, lengthening his neck and straightening his knees. He towers over us both, his eyes flashing, but Uziyah could break his thin form without blinking. Salam's haughty sniff communicates his displeasure.

"He reminds me of religious fanatics back home," I say. "The sense of entitlement. Controlling people with shame and guilt. Endless judgement and penance. But when you finally stand against them, they're spineless."

I press my lips together when I finish speaking, careful to only breathe through my nose.

Wouldn't that be a laugh if I accidentally inhaled the gas?

"Do not compare me to savages," Salam snaps.

"You're the most savage of all." I draw the knife from my sleeve. "Walk to the control room. And I mean that last part—*walk*."

Salam spins on his heel, his wings narrowly missing me and Uziyah. He stalks into the corridor and we follow a couple of steps behind. Salam is a dark and grizzled vulture in the bright and gleaming space.

"How have you corrupted yet another of our Protectorate?" he says after five minutes of furious stomping. "It should not be possible with one such as Uziyah. He is a perfect specimen. *Was* a perfect specimen."

"Blame your own brutality. Hunter battered him around the head and damaged the cybernetics. Turns out when you dial down the aggression, he's not such an arsehole."

"Thank you, feeble creature," Uziyah says.

Salam tuts but stays silent. His head hunches low, disappearing behind his wings.

His leg snaps out and pistons backwards, his torso horizontal. His foot catches Uziyah in the chest and Uziyah stumbles, colliding with the wall. A two-thumbed palm swings for me. I catch Salam's forearm by reflex.

It's not the first time I've been slapped on this godforsaken ship. My jaw still aches from the burn of Abayankari's backhand.

Salam claws for the command hubs despite the knife in my grip. Uziyah growls behind me. Salam jerks away, a nick on his wrist for his troubles. His wings flare. My hand punches out. The blade slices the leathery skin between delicate bones. Salam shrieks and flaps harder, gaining height. I slice again. Silver blood splatters the pearly walls.

Froth but no super-sealing.

Salam collapses, his torn wings shivering. Uziyah hauls him up and shoves him forward, a broad hand clamped on his scrawny bicep.

"She told you to walk. You did not walk." Uziyah smiles gleefully. "I hope you have learned your lesson."

We lead a subdued Salam to the control centre without further incident. He leaves droplets of blood in the corridor, like a scattering of silver pennies. We pass the unconscious Riot and leave him where he fell.

Steph, Greg and Bronwyn stand on the raised dais, staring at the screens. They turn as we enter through the open doorway. Our reflections follow us in the gleaming dome of the roof.

"Maia! Thank god you're all right," Steph says, then after a slight pause, "and, uh, you too, Uziyah."

Uziyah rewards her with a tiny incline of his head. Salam's bright gaze sweeps the room, lingering on Bronwyn and the trussed Tallai lying on a floating stretcher. The harsh violet of Tallai's eyes is dulled beneath a filmy membrane.

"You will be executed for this, Bronwyn'challi," Salam says, his voice cold and buzzing. "To die by your own hand is too honourable for one such as you."

Bronwyn's wings droop. I open my mouth to defend her but she straightens her shoulders and meets the gaze of the older Creator.

"Punishment and subjugation should not be the accepted methods for controlling other universes, or the Protectorate. They have served us for many of our lifetimes. They deserve the right to choose their fate."

"Idiot youngling," Salam snarls. "You have brought shame on our province by colluding with a barbaric race and betraying your own kind for worthless ideals."

"Barbaric race," I snort, and earn a smirk from Steph.

Bronwyn folds her hands, her eyes calm. "To end the suffering and cruelty is not worthless. We have overstepped in our role here. We grew too bold, too greedy for power, with the strength of the Protectorate behind us. Humanity has shown it is time to change. Time to relinquish control of the warriors we made."

"Humanity and all the others who are a stain on their solar systems will be brought to heel. I will not allow our province to be the only one to fail in that mission." Salam's voice rises. "The Protectorate are ours to use as we see fit until the end of all time. That is the way it has always been and always will be."

"Isn't it about *time* we shut this bastard up?" Steph mutters.

Greg holds out his hand, and Steph slaps it. The tubing of the respirators loop between their nostrils. Like Salam, Bronwyn's tubing curves over her beak.

Uziyah clamps a hand on Salam's shoulder. "Kneel."

The word sends an uncomfortable frisson in my gut.

The Creator resists. Uziyah's muscles bulge, and Salam folds into a crouch. Bronwyn flutters her wings and sails off the dais, walking the last few steps. Reluctance screams through her movements. She holds a roll of bandages out to Uziyah.

"Restrain him," she says. "Please."

Salam scoffs. "A Creator does not ask. They *command*."

"They should ask. And they should beg forgiveness of an intelligent, self-aware race they have abused for aeons."

Go, Bronwyn!

I curl my fingers instead of offering her a high-five. She wouldn't know what it means.

Uziyah regards her, his sooty eyes intense, then he dips into a graceful bow despite his bulk. He plucks the bandages from her hand.

"Hold up." Greg jumps off the dais, pausing only long enough to assist Steph, who gives him a fond eye roll. He hops to us, yanking off his shoe and his remaining sock. "Got another gag for him. Sounds like he needs it."

"Insolent human," Salam sneers from his crouched position. "Your life will be short and unpleasant."

My blade taps his beak, making a satisfying *clack-clack*. He startles and sits on his knees. His gaze zips to me.

"You're not in power anymore, Salam," I say. "How about you take *that* with grace, hmm?"

He bares his teeth. "My name is Salam—*gack!*"

Greg punches his sock into the Creator's mouth. Uziyah wraps the bandage around then binds Salam's wrists, wings and ankles until he's as trussed as the blessedly silent Tallai. Salam thrashes but his complaints are muffled.

"Should we pluck out his respirator and really shut him up?" Steph says, eyeballing the Creator with distaste.

I shake my head. "Keep him awake for now. If he behaves and tells us how to steer the ship, maybe I won't hand him over to the human authorities to be punished."

Salam narrows his bright gaze at me.

Greg grins wide. "I can't believe we're going to captain a spaceship. Can I have a go?"

"We'll see," I say, and turn to Bronwyn. "How long will the gas keep the angels unconscious?"

"I am maintaining a steady sedative concentration but I would not recommend using it longer than one planetary circuit. The Protectorate's metabolism is able to adapt and counteract if they are exposed to it for long periods. Then it becomes ineffective and a new gas must be deployed."

"Did Salam communicate with anyone outside of the ship?"

Salam increases his glare, which answers my question, though Bronwyn says, "No, child. The ship's log shows no external communication, either planetary or between vessels."

Greg bounces on his toes, one foot bare since he's forgotten to put his shoe back on. "How many Protectorate ships are out there?"

"In our province? Four others are in orbit. Six are on assignment in different universes."

"Poor bastards," Greg says.

I assume he means the inhabitants of the unruly planets and not the Protectorate no doubt slaughtering their way through them.

"What forms are the others?" Greg continues, bouncing a little more. "Maia said they were all supposed to be different to the angels. I'd love to see—"

"Greg…" I sigh.

He holds up his hands. "Right. *Shut up, Greg.* Sorry."

Steph throws an arm across his shoulders. "You're such a geek."

He smiles, unabashed, and puts his arm around her waist. His cheeks glow pink when he meets my gaze.

"How long do we have until someone notices there's been a coup on this ship?" I ask Bronwyn.

She cocks her head. "We are due to be relieved for a cycle of rest in twenty-three planetary circuits. We will not be disturbed if we continue to send the expected reports, unless there is a call for deployment to another universe."

A tension in my chest eases. I pace beside Salam, tracked by his annoyed gaze. Uziyah watches the Creator, though he's not going anywhere.

"So we have some time." I spin on my heel. "Bronwyn—stay here and guard Salam and Tallai. Feel free to keep telling Salam how wrong he is about everything. Steph, Greg and Uziyah—come with me. We have about ten thousand angels to put in stasis tubes."

"Look at her," Steph whispers. "She's being all leadery again."

Greg throws me a jaunty salute. "We're with you, Angeltamer. All the way."

We troop out, turfing Tallai off his floating stretcher and directed by Bronwyn to where we can get more. Uziyah pulls ahead, though it's more purposeful stride than angry stomp for once. Steph holds Greg's hand but doesn't appear to notice. Greg keeps grinning at their entwined fingers like the lovesick puppy he is.

It warms my fractured heart to see it. To know that if the worst happens, if we never get our angels back to who they

were before, Steph will have Greg. As for me…
I'm trying not to think about it.

28

Dark lashes sweep the planes of Hunter's cheekbones, tangled in the hair falling across his forehead. His face is relaxed in his chemically induced coma. No snarl or sneer or thirst for violence.

He looks like my Hunter.

I try to remember how he was before—gentle, a calm and steady presence, his eager hands and sexy possessiveness—instead of thinking about him pinning me to the wall, the pain and terror. The violation.

Seems I'm thinking about it anyway.

Steph stops petting Devinon's hair where he's sprawled on a stretcher, floating above the scattered bodies he was extricated from, the rest still piled around the arena. His sapphire wings trail to the ground. She picks her way carefully to me, leaving Greg to guard their sleeping angel.

"We'll get him back," she says softly. "We'll get them all back."

I manage a nod, playing the silky black feathers of Hunter's wings through my fingers. The sensory memory of them sweeping across my skin, tickling and teasing, gathers a sob in the base of my throat.

It wasn't just a sex thing. Hunter loved to do it when I read to him, cuddled in his arms. It was tender, soothing. Comfort and closeness.

"I hope he doesn't remember," I croak, and raise my gaze. "He hurt me, Steph. He'll never forgive himself."

"As long as you forgive him, that's all that matters."

"I will." I swallow hard. "I mean—I do."

She pulls me to my feet from my crouched position. "Let's get him loaded up. The quicker we pack them away, the quicker we get out of here. I want to go home."

What faith she has. I still have no idea how we're going to steer the spaceship if Salam proves unhelpful.

We roll Hunter onto his back, partly on top of the angel next to him. I jam my hands under his shoulders while Steph grabs his feet. Together, we hoist him onto a stretcher and manoeuvre his wings to flop on either side. His shirt rides up to flash a smooth line of stomach. My heart kicks. I suck air through my nose despite the exertion.

Greg guides Dev across the arena, lining the two angels up side by side—one bright blue, one black. Both lovely in repose.

"You guys take those two," Greg says. "I'll grab another and follow you."

Uziyah dives over a balcony and lands in a cleared space. He scoops Markian and Abayankari under his arms, the warriors limp and drooping. His legs bunch, propelling him upwards.

"You humans are so slow at everything," he says, his sneer a gentle mockery of its former self.

His wings flap hard. He swoops over another balcony and out of sight. The ferns shiver in his wake.

"Show off," Steph mutters.

Since we humans also don't have wings to get out of this cursed arena, we clamber onto the foot of our respective stretchers and slowly float them higher. I find myself gripping

Hunter's shin, my other hand on the stretcher's controls embedded in the edge of the contraption. I squeeze the familiar stiffness of his laced boot over the firmness of bone and muscle.

My stretcher bonks into a spectator box with an awful clang. I wobble on my knees, vertigo hollowing my gut. My grip on Hunter's leg threatens to break it.

Similar to how he broke mine.

The stretcher scrapes upwards. I grit my teeth against the screech, and jab at the buttons. The machine ploughs through the ferns in a waft of mushrooms and mulch. I hop off, shaky and relieved to be on solid ground. Steph jumps next to me. We steer our precious cargo into the corridor. Greg trails us with a bang and a curse.

Uziyah flits overhead, smirking and empty-handed. He passes us twice more by the time we reach the boxy sleeping rooms full of pallets, even though they're not far from the arena. Wall panels have popped open to reveal rows of vertical glass tubes and their cushions of gelatinous pink. Unlike the shuttle, the stasis pods occupy every level right up to the roof.

Thankfully, Uziyah is filling those.

We line up our stretchers to the three closest tubes. Getting the angels in the pods takes a lot of grunting and sweating and false starts until I just grab Hunter around the chest, my hands locked between his wings, and drag him into the tube. I stumble over his legs and slam him into the rear of the pod with a splat, my nose pressed to his pec. I can't smell his clean, icy scent through the respirator.

At least he's light and not a total whale like Uziyah.

I tuck his wings around him, and step back. He sags a little but the goop keeps him upright, cradling his body. The door hisses shut. Pinkness creeps across the black of his feathers and covers his hands. Steph bumps her shoulder into mine, Greg next to her, and we stare at our angels encased in pink. They breathe quiet and smooth while we huff through our nostrils.

"And we only have to do that about a thousand more times," Greg says cheerfully.

Steph and I groan.

* * *

Moving the angelic Protectorate into the stasis pods takes the full planetary rotation. Thankfully, not all of the warriors were in the arena like I first assumed. About two thirds of them followed their programming and tucked themselves into the tubes. Uziyah does about ninety percent of the remaining angels himself without stopping to rest, snorting at us poor humans when we sag to the floor for another break to ease our aching bones and muscles. Shifting bodies and not being able to breathe through our mouths feels like suffocating. We also can't risk falling asleep, not even for a power nap.

Bronwyn stays in the control room to monitor the comms systems and talk to Salam, who alternates between cajoling mumbles and furious screeches behind his gag. She uses the screens to scan the rest of the ship and point out the locations of scattered angels who weren't in the arena to watch my final battle with Hunter and Abayankari but didn't make it to the pods.

Steph, Greg and I load the last angel, collapsing into a sweaty and exhausted heap on the floor. Uziyah stands over us, his hands on his hips, but tiredness dulls his eyes and droops his gold-tinged wings.

"Would you tell Bronwyn to turn off the gas?" I say, unable to lift my head from Steph's stomach.

Greg is a tangle of limbs and hair beside me, propped on Steph's chest and staring at the ceiling, his eyes half-lidded.

Uziyah cants his head. "As you wish, feeble creature."

He zips out the door in a flash of sunflower yellow.

"He's just taking the piss now, isn't he?" Steph says.

"Looks like it."

I bite my lip to stifle a yawn, and my eyes water.

"God, I can't wait to get these plugs out of my nose," Steph huffs.

Greg nods, bouncing on Steph's boob. He yawns wide enough to crack his jaw, and sucks in a whoop of air. Steph meets my startled gaze over the top of him.

Greg wrinkles his lip. "What tastes like death?"

It takes him a second, the genius that he is. Panic flashes in his eyes.

"Oh, shit," he says, and collapses.

29

"You're an idiot," I say in greeting when Greg stumbles into the control room, pale and tired despite his impromptu nap.

I guess his body is used to chemicals by now, though huffing sedative gas is a little different to smoking weed. Probably.

Steph got her hands on a cannabis brownie once. I spent the night shrieking with laughter and talking nonsense. Time had no meaning. My tongue felt weird.

Greg gives me a sheepish grin. "Could've happened to the best of us."

Steph slides from her perch beside the surprisingly compact control panel in the centre of the dais. She strolls down the ramp, her casual gait marred by a slight limp. Her reflection chases her in the silver dome of the ceiling.

Next to me, Bronwyn and Uziyah track her progress, their attention tugged from the many screens on the walls. My nostrils ache from the intrusion of the respirator, now tucked away in a pouch on Bronwyn's belt.

The trussed Salam has finally exhausted himself and stopped wriggling in Uziyah's grip. Tallai, however, has been energised since the dissipation of the gas and keeps expressing his displeasure with snorts and muffled whines from his position on the floor.

Steph captures Greg's chin in her hand and looks down into his face. "How are you feeling?"

She panicked when he collapsed, fluttering over him like the pet name Dev uses for her. She threw herself on top of him to press an ear to his chest. She even started giving him mouth to mouth before I eased her away since he was breathing fine. She was more likely to join him in unconsciousness on a forgetful whoop of air. Instead, she peppered his cheeks with kisses and called him 'prickles' and 'stupid fucking idiot'.

She's definitely in love.

"I'm okay," Greg says quietly. "Woozy. I had the weirdest dreams."

Steph grabs him into a tight hug. Greg appears to be suffocating in her boobs but he doesn't complain.

"Don't scare me like that again," she says into his mussed hair.

He nods, and she releases him. Redness blooms in his face. He ducks his head to hide but I don't miss the delight tugging at his mouth. I turn back to the console to distract myself from the tight heat in my chest.

Devinon deserves to share the affection they have for each other. He deserves to be loved by them both after a lifetime on this cold and brutal ship. And Hunter...

The tightness creeps to my throat.

I swallow past it. "Bronwyn, can you programme this thing to travel to Earth? Or even just get us through the wormhole?"

"Alas, child, I cannot. My experience lies with the communication system, not navigation."

Salam chokes behind his gag, his severe eyes narrow and mocking. I frown at the console. The entire control system for the Protectorate ship is contained within a single screen of incomprehensible symbols. A large version of the two command hubs weighing down my wrist. No levers, no dials. Not even a joystick.

I grew up with Spectrum and Atari courtesy of the neighbourhood boys—I could've handled a joystick.

I look at Uziyah but he shakes his head. "Weapons are taken to where they are needed. They are never in control. And I cannot read the Creator language."

"Okay," I sigh. "Remove his gag."

Uziyah unwraps the bandage around Salam's beak and plucks Greg's soggy sock from the Creator's gob. His hand returns to Salam's bicep to hold him in place, the Creator unsteady on his feet with his stork legs bound together. Salam's shredded but clotted wings twitch against the bandages.

"Your penance for this will be swift and merciless." He snaps his beak. "All of you will suffer. All of you will—"

I poke the tip of my knife into his arm. He hisses and tries to jerk away but the bulk of Uziyah blocks him. A silver bead of blood glides down to stain a strip of bandage.

"Worry about your own suffering," I say. "Tell me how to get this ship to Earth."

Uziyah shoves Salam closer to the console. I side-step to give him room. Steph and Greg join me in their wrinkled wedding finery, all of us clustered around the controls, the rest of the ship silent and still.

Salam glares out of one baleful eye. "I will tell you nothing, human. Enjoy the last moments of your freedom. Soon, I will crush it."

"He really is a downer, isn't he?" Greg mutters.

I poke Salam's arm again. More silver mars the bandage. He bares his pointy teeth.

"Go ahead—torture me. Slaughter me in cold blood like the savage you are."

Tallai cackles beneath his gag but we ignore him.

"You torture and slaughter more than humanity ever has," I say, struggling to keep my voice steady. "You cross universes to do it, for goodness' sake."

My hand shakes, the blade held clear of Salam's flesh to avoid carving him up. The trouble is, I want to. I want to stab my knife into his rough and pitted skin. I want to slash and slice until he's a mewling puddle of exposed and shivering tissue. After everything he's done, it would be so easy to cross that line and match his brutality with my own. My blood *sings* for it.

But killing in battle is one thing. I won't let the Creators turn me into a creature as cruel as their whole race. Violence is never the way.

"We judge and punish as they deserve," Salam sneers.

"There's no talking to him, Maia." Steph's expression matches the Creator's. "Psychopaths can't be reasoned with."

Uziyah spreads his wings, his flight feathers brushing the screens on the wall that show the rest of the vessel. "Let me do it. Let me hurt him."

Salam lunges at Uziyah but the angel watches him with a stony gaze and refuses to flinch. Salam's beak snaps on air.

"Ungrateful wretch. You will be broken and remade into the tool you are meant to be. You will be honoured to follow my commands."

I rub my gritty eyes. "They rule through pain and fear. We don't. Put his gag back on. How hard can it be to drive an advanced, alien spaceship? It's only a little bigger than my Mitsubishi."

"You will fail," Salam hisses. "You will perish. You will—"

Salam tosses his head, dodging the loop of bandage in Uziyah's hand. His sharp beak scrapes a bloodless furrow down Uziyah's forearm. He wrenches from Uziyah's hold. Starts to topple.

A hand whips out. Long fingers, two thumbs, the flapping and ragged ends of a bandage slowly unravelling.

I'm not fast enough this time.

The crack of a slap. The crack of my neck. Both seem to echo inside and out.

I'm on the floor, though I don't remember falling. Steph screams my name. Greg screams it, too.

An inferno of pain licks along my jawbone. I try to touch my face, assess the damage, but nothing happens. There's an emptiness below my neck. An absence. I can't move. I can't do anything but blink at the same patch of shiny floor, and breathe.

My air stutters. Or my chest, but I can't feel it.

Can I breathe?

I can't breathe.

30

I wake wrapped in the shroud on my usual slab. It's preferable to the tank of pink goo.

I pray this is the last time I'm in the healing ward, though if we manage to steer the ship to Earth and not explode into a ball of fiery death, the Global Protection Alliance will want to replicate the technology.

"Maia, thank god!"

Steph grabs my hand, Greg crowded next to her. Relief fizzes through my gut.

I can feel her palm in mine, gripping it hard. I can feel my toes, my knees, my chest. A faint ache throbs in my neck and jaw and I welcome that, too.

"Same goes for you," Steph continues. "Don't scare me like that. Both of you will be the death of me."

Greg pats my arm. "You scared the shit out of me, too, man. But this healing stuff is amazing."

Steph rolls her eyes. "You missed the last two hours of Greg quizzing Bronwyn on every piece of technology in this room and beyond. I was so bored, I almost wished *my* neck was broken."

"You fell asleep after I asked the first question," Greg says. "You were snoring in my lap."

Steph scoffs. "I do *not* snore. I may snort, occasionally, like a lady."

"Or a chainsaw," Greg whispers to me. "It's adorable."

Bronwyn unwraps the shroud from my throat, her gentle fingers kneading my skin. "How are you feeling, child?"

"Better. Where's Uziyah?"

"The Hulk is guarding those overgrown lizards," Steph says while Bronwyn returns the healing shroud to its misty glass ball. "They're knotted up tighter than that set of Christmas lights you insist on untangling every year."

She helps me sit up, assisted by Greg, and I swing my legs over the edge of the slab.

"Maybe it'll be Christmas by the time we get home."

Steph smirks. "Then I can't wait to watch you growl at that ball of lights for half an hour while Hunter watches as if you're the most fascinating thing in the world."

His name, and the fond memory, is a punch to the heart. After she left that day, he tied me to the bed with the twinkling fairy lights. He played with me for *hours*. When he finally let me come, I reached a higher plane of existence that was a million times better than any religious heaven.

I'll never throw those lights out.

I clear my throat. "They have sentimental value."

I slide gingerly to my feet, and balance between Steph and Greg. Bronwyn looks on with her hands folded.

"If we do make it back, we'll probably have missed at least one Christmas," Greg says, somehow still cheerfully.

"Way to ruin the mood, prickles," Steph says.

We traipse back to the control room through the empty and eerie corridors, the bright colours hurting my eyes. Tiredness dulls my senses, my movements sluggish. The constant trauma and grief and healing probably don't help.

Uziyah stands over Salam and Tallai, both now on the floor at the base of the ramp. I can barely see a strip of grey flesh between the layer of bandages, topped by some kind of braided wire torn at the ends and tied in a bow at their butts. Uziyah's gaze snaps to mine as I shuffle through the doorway. He meets me half-way and drops to his knees.

"Forgive me, feeble creature." His hair sweeps forward as he lowers his head, his wings arched behind him. "It is my fault you were hurt."

My tentative fingers touch his bent head. "Don't kneel for me, Uziyah. You don't have to kneel ever again. Well… unless you want to."

He peeks at me through a curtain of sunflower-yellow. "Why would I choose to kneel?"

"Uh…"

Steph smirks. "Oh, this should be as good as you trying to explain love to Hunter."

Nope. I'm not talking oral sex with another angel. Been there, done that.

"You'll figure it out when you get to Earth and see how consensual relationships work," I say.

Steph opens her mouth but I slide her a look and she shuts it, her smirk widening into a grin. Uziyah climbs to his feet, still frowning. We gather around the trussed Creators. Salam and Tallai strain their necks to glare at us from their severe, fluorescent eyes.

"What are we going to do with Tweedle-dee and Tweedle-dinosaur?" Steph plants her fists on her silk-clad hips. "I vote for blasting them out into the void where they belong."

"They're not going to tell us how to operate the ship, not that we can trust what they say, anyway. No doubt they'll signal for help given the opportunity. I do like this blasting them into space idea." I focus on Bronwyn opposite me. "Is there an escape pod we can put them in?"

"There is an emergency vessel, yes," Bronwyn says over Salam's furious buzzing. "It is a single vehicle designed to hold the full crew of three from a Protectorate ship."

A smile stretches my mouth. It feels a little evil.

"Lead the way," I say.

We load the Creators onto two floating stretchers and follow Bronwyn through the labyrinthine corridors to the bowels of the ship. Salam and Tallai screech and squirm but Uziyah's firm hand on their backs keeps them from wriggling off. Bronwyn splays her palm on a patch of wall indistinguishable to the rest. A rectangular doorway whooshes open to a short, transparent corridor. We hustle our captives one by one into a dark vessel shaped like a teardrop. Uziyah dumps them on the floor in the centre of a trio of chairs. A window above a control screen looks out onto stars, the Creators' planet on the other side of the Protectorate ship behind us, along with the sun and the moons. Interstellar traffic zips in regimented lines across the velvet infinity.

"Do you have the stuff that passes for food in here?" I say.

Bronwyn taps the wall. A rack of familiar beakers clinks out. Uziyah holds the Creators' beaks open while I pour the mixture down their throats. They squawk and splutter. Uziyah gags them again before Salam can prophesy our doom. I crouch next to Salam. Tears magnify the colour of his eyes, blazing violet with his hatred.

"You've received the last of my mercy," I say quietly, holding his gaze. "Remember that if you get free and decide to seek me out."

I straighten and turn on my bare heel, striding into the corridor without looking back.

31

Controlling the Protectorate ship is, unfortunately, not like playing a super-fancy, touch-screen video game. It's an overwhelming responsibility that puts the lives of my best friends, my husband, my allies and thousands of other angels in my hands. Not exactly great when I haven't slept properly today—or the whole time I've been here—and my muscles throb from lugging bodies around. A headache sizzles between my temples and down my spine. My shoulders are so tense, they brush my ears.

Bronwyn has translated the incomprehensible symbols on the screen of the control panel but it's nothing as simple as stop and start or even forward and back. It's all about percentage of thrust and angle of trajectory and some gobbledegook algorithm for escape velocity. My first attempts spun us around and set off a bunch of alarms before I sent us on some kind of hyper-drive straight into the sun. We spent a fraught few minutes waiting to see if our movements alerted anyone in our orbit.

Salam is no doubt cackling into his gag. But it's only another sign of their arrogance that, despite their advanced technology, no one has interrupted our takeover.

Yet.

Sweat drips into my eye. I curse at the sting and scrub my face on the sleeve of my bodysuit.

Bronwyn got me a fresh one. It's bigger than the last so the crotch hangs past my knees. I look ridiculous. Steph and Greg chose to stay in their wedding clothes. Bronwyn kept my dress but it made me too sad to put it back on.

Steph touches a hand to my back. I hope she can't feel me shaking.

"You got this, Maia," she says softly, no hint of reproach or frustration in her voice.

If I were her, I'd be shitting myself.

Wait. I *am* shitting myself. This is so much worse than driving my Mitsubishi into battle in the middle of the apocalypse.

Steph and Greg are standing behind me, offering (mostly) silent support and trying not to be a distraction. Uziyah is patrolling the ship, restless and not so great at being quiet. Bronwyn peers at the screen next to me. She keeps wringing her hands and flicking her wings. It's not helping my nerves. I'm dizzy, weak, exhausted. Heart-sick and traumatised.

I really shouldn't be piloting a spaceship.

"You still want a shot, Greg?" I say somewhat hopefully.

He clears his throat. "Nah, man, I'm good. I trust you."

Dammit.

I wish Hunter were here. He'd promise me something amazing to bribe me into moving. Something I could do to him, or he'd do to me. Generally sexual but not always. He'd know what to say to calm me down.

I suck in a breath. Roll my aching shoulders. Fidget. My finger hovers over the squiggle that means 'execute'.

"Fifth time's the charm," I whisper, and tap the screen.

Symbols flash as my calculations are initiated by the computer. I can't feel the movement of the ship, only watch the monitor now showing the vastness of space. The stars stay where they are. The screen emits a bleat of displeasure.

"We need that paperclip thing," Greg says. "'It looks like you're trying to pilot an intergalactic spaceship. Need some help?'"

A hysterical giggle lodges in my throat. I dare not let it out in case the laughter turns to shrieking.

I point at a shape blinking in the corner of the screen. It looks like a square, a triangle and a diamond all had a baby. "What's that?"

Bronwyn leans closer. She touches the symbol and it opens a new page of scrolling script. Her cheeks darken.

"My apologies, child. This is a log of all previous calculations. I did not see the option before." She taps the final line of script. "This should be the last command that was programmed."

Greg squeaks behind me. "Did I just conjure the spaceship equivalent of Mr Clippy?"

Steph shushes him. I stare at the screen, anxiety churning in my gut. The calculation Bronwyn tapped sits at the top, other symbols scattered around the border.

"So, in theory, I just need to reverse the calculation? Do any of these buttons mean that?"

Bronwyn's finger hovers above a dollar sign turned on its side in the centre of a spiky circle. "This is the closest translation—rewind."

"How funny," I mutter. "I would like to rewind this entire period of my life."

I press the symbol before I can talk myself out of it. The stars on the monitor shift.

"We're moving," Steph breathes.

I don't need to glance behind me to know she and Greg are hugging. I cuddle my elbows to my chest, my body chilled.

Why is it so bloody cold on this ship?

"How will we know we're going the right way?" I ask no one in particular. "What does a wormhole even look like?"

"Actually, we won't be able to see the wormhole," Greg says. "It's supposed to be a black hole in the blackness of space. When we're in it, we might be able to notice a tunnel shape, and maybe some kind of distortion at the end. Or nothing at all. In theory."

"Great," I say. "So we just see where we end up and hope we don't die."

Silence falls in the silent ship. We watch the stars drift. My heart slams against my ribs, the ebb and flow of adrenaline leaving me nauseated and woozy.

"You figured it out."

We all jump at Uziyah's voice, even Bronwyn. He looms behind Steph and Greg.

"Christ's sake, Uziyah," I say past the heart twitching in my mouth, "wear a bell next time."

He tilts his head. "Why would I wear a bell?"

"Never mind. Do you know if we're going in the right direction?"

"Yes, feeble creature. This is the trajectory taken when we were first assigned to subjugate Earth."

My hand flaps at the air instead of gripping the console and triggering some kind of self-destruct. Steph grabs my arm and tucks me into her side before my knees give out.

The stars streak, then disappear. My heart returns to my mouth. There's no tunnel, no distortion—whatever the hell that means. My eyes mist. I try to blink it clear but it stays.

Chunks of rock and the infinity of dots and clouds replace the nothingness.

Greg whoops. My poor heart nearly stops beating. The rest of me is about ready to collapse.

"The Oort Cloud," he says. "It's the fucking Oort Cloud!"

Steph squeezes me against her side until I can feel the press of her ribs. "You did it, Maia. I knew you would."

"We're still a long, *long* way from Earth," I croak. "And this ship has never been there."

The screen bleeps. Bronwyn chuckles before I have a chance to panic.

"'You have entered the Milky Way galaxy,'" she reads, trailing her finger along the garbled text. "'Journey time to the nearest inhabited planet is one hundred and forty-six planetary rotations. Do you wish to proceed?'"

"You bet your arse we wish to proceed," Steph yells.

She dances Greg around the dais despite her worsening limp and somehow ropes Uziyah into giving her a twirl. Bronwyn gestures at the screen.

I point where she's pointing, and hesitate. "Definitely this button here?" I lower my hand a fraction, still hesitating. "Definitely this one?"

"Yes, child. That is the button."

I jab it so hard, I hurt my finger. Steph spins me around, dips me and plants a big, smacking kiss on my lips. She parks me back at the console before I can blink.

"Right, ah… How do I eject the escape pod?"

Bronwyn's eyes crinkle in amusement but she bends to the screen. "I saw a menu while we were searching earlier. Here— this will eject the escape pod."

"It won't stop our course for Earth, will it?"

"I do not think so, child. Not when triggered from the control room."

I press the button without further hesitation. No blip of guilt, either.

Salam and Tallai are getting what *they* deserve.

"You're firing them into the Oort Cloud?" Greg stops beside me in a breathless tangle with Steph.

"No better place for them than to drift among the rest of the space rubbish," I say.

Steph holds out her fist, and I bump it.

"Good riddance," she says.

I crane around Steph to see Greg. "How long is a hundred and forty-six planetary rotations, anyway?"

"One planetary rotation is two and a half of our days so a hundred and forty-six…" He looks at the ceiling, a finger tapping his bottom lip. "…is a year."

"A year!"

"Holy shit," Steph says. "No wonder they take the shuttle. Should we take the shuttle?"

I shake my head. "We need to get them all to Earth and I don't fancy transferring thousands of bodies to shuttles, if there are even enough to hold them. Plus the GPA are going to want this ship."

"So, we sleep?" Greg says.

I turn to Bronwyn. "Will the ship wake us when we arrive?"

She glides down the ramp to a section of wall. A panel opens to reveal three transparent tubes, the pink goo ready and waiting.

"These stasis pods are tuned to the ship's system. The rest are roused manually."

Greg salutes us with a finger. "Ladies first. Uziyah and I can find a spare tube. Uh, I mean a spare two tubes. Sweet dreams, everyone."

"See you in a year, I guess," I say.

Greg smiles. "It'll only feel like a minute."

Uziyah strides from the room, followed by Greg.

"I'd better go tuck him in," Steph says, and scuttles after them both.

Bronwyn fusses at the entrance to a tube, folding her wings tight to her back and reversing in. She pauses when she catches me watching her.

"Are you nervous about coming with us?" I say. "I never asked you if you wanted to live on Earth."

She crosses her hands against her concave chest. "I knew this would be the eventuality when you asked for my aid. I admit, I am curious about your home world. They accepted the Protectorate who remained behind. I hope it means they will accept me, too."

"They will."

"Then I am not nervous."

She sinks into the goo and closes her eyes. The curved glass door slides shut. Pinkness swallows the pastel in her wings and creeps over her pale-grey skin. Steph hurries in a few minutes later.

"They're in a room just down the corridor," she says. "All tucked in and covered in goop."

I nod, though I'm only half-listening.

Maybe I should have kept Salam and Tallai onboard and shoved them in a stasis pod to keep them out of trouble. They'll free themselves eventually, cutting the bandages with the rough edge of their beaks. What if they intercept us before we get home? What if I open my eyes to their gloating faces and a fate more horrific than what I've already endured? What if—

"Hey," Steph says, and I jump. "Take a deep breath, Maia."

My ribs strain against my gulp of air.

"What if we can't cure our angels?" I blurt. "What if the GPA has built a powerful weapon that blows us to smithereens as soon as we reach the moon? We'll have been gone for almost two years. Two *years,* Steph."

She grips my shoulders, forcing me to raise my gaze to her face instead of frowning at the floor.

"One step at a time." She guides my hand, the one with the wedding rings, until the bands press over my heart. "You've fought this hard for him. You just need to fight a little longer. But you're not fighting alone."

"Thanks, Steph," I whisper. "I don't know what I'd do without you."

She tucks a curl of hair behind my ear, and smiles. "You'd be bored to tears."

We settle into our tubes. I press my palm to the glass and Steph covers it on her side. Pink goo tickles my cheeks. I shut my eyes.

The throb of the ship's engines fades. Consciousness fades. I huff the scent of oranges and catch my final thought before the goo swallows it.

We're going home…

… I hope.

32

"I'm not sure about this."

My hushed voice fills the observation room. Fluorescent lights reflect off the harsh, white walls and the lab coat of the operator. Her wheeled chair squeaks as she shifts, her desk crowded by a semi-circle of monitors. Through the glass, the hulking machine awaits her command. The black soles of a pair of boots are all that's visible in the circular opening.

Steph squeezes my hand while leaning on her cane. Her pink wig curls past her shoulders, a shade lighter than her wool jumper. "Uziyah did it and look at him—he's fine."

The bulk of Uziyah and the spread of his wings turn the already narrow space into a cramped box. He treats me to an upnod—a human gesture he's learned in the two months we've been on Earth. His favourite is giving people the finger.

"I am fine, feeble creature," he says. "It did not hurt."

He volunteered to be the first to use the MRI machine despite the failure of the last couple of methods.

Semi-invincible warrior angels can die if their brains melt. Who knew?

We lost two—Riot and another white-winged Protectorate— to EMP and electric shock when they made the cybernetics spark. It was awful to watch their convulsions. The scientists in charge acted as if it was normal to lose test subjects while guilt ravaged my stomach and shot bile into my throat. Of course, I had to be the one to pick the sacrifices. Random selection made it fair but I won't forget my relief when it wasn't Hunter or Dev or any of our Jewels.

And I have to live with that.

I also had to swallow my instinctive refusal of Uziyah's selfless offer—I've grown fond of the big brute—and hide a tear or two. He finally has the freedom to live as he chooses yet he risked it all for the greater good. He could have died, twitching and rigid, like the other two. Instead, the cybernetics seemed to shrivel from thermal induction in the leads.

Greg squeezes my other hand where I'm sandwiched between him and Steph. "It'll work, Maia."

He's back to his usual smell of weed instead of biscuits. It's comforting. When we finally got home to Martello Court after a whirlwind week of interrogations, medical exams and emergency meetings, smog filled his flat for days. You could see it puffing out the air vents, for goodness' sake. Steph and I needed oxygen masks just to enter.

"I'm ready to begin," the operator says softly.

Her black hair in a ponytail dangles to the small of her back. I've forgotten her name—Doctor Rashmi or Rasheem. Something like that. She sneaks a glance at Uziyah then hunkers closer to her keyboard.

The WACO team nearly filled him full of iron when we stepped off the Protectorate ship. It'll take a lot more than my word before people trust the white- or golden-winged varieties. Bronwyn, on the other hand, was welcomed with a surge of curiosity. She's off being tested elsewhere in the government facility.

She seems to enjoy the attention.

The ship woke us when we approached Earth, just as she said it would. It was like I'd only closed my eyes for a second but a whole year had passed. We stumbled from our respective tubes, groggy and weak. Steph woke Greg and Uziyah and we all downed a beaker of tart glop for what I hoped would be the last time. I almost spat it right back out when alarms blared through the control room.

Turns out, the GPA *had* built a better defence system in the time we were gone and the damn thing shot at us. If it were up to me to activate the shield, we'd all be dust drifting in space but the ship protected itself automatically. It also blasted the no doubt expensive satellite into tiny, glittering pieces.

That was a little embarrassing.

We managed to communicate our intent via radio waves. We never got a reply but the other defensive satellites crowding our orbit didn't fire on us so someone must have heard.

I was tempted to drift around in space until proper astronauts came to our rescue but a menu popped up on the control screen. All we needed were coordinates.

"What about Arthur's Seat?" Greg said.

"How do you have coordinates for Arthur's Seat?"

Greg shrugged. "I like to geocache."

"Such a geek," Steph said.

I programmed the latitude and longitude into the computer and our self-parking spaceship plummeted to Earth in a trail of fire and smoke. The black and foreboding Protectorate ship crunched on top of Arthur's Seat on the evening of November 25th, changing the view of Edinburgh into a sci-fi fan's wet dream and casting a permanent shadow over the buildings below, including the Scottish Parliament. The blazing lights of jets and helicopters filled the night sky. Tanks rumbled in the streets. We stumbled out of a transparent tunnel onto rocky scree. Freezing rain whipped around the crags. The air smelled of damp stone and something sweet.

What a sight we must have been, blinking into the glare of spotlights—three humans, two dressed for a wedding and one in an unflattering bodysuit, a terrifying warrior angel and a creature that looked like a cross between a dinosaur and a vulture.

No offence to Bronwyn.

The WACO team stormed the slopes. After I convinced them not to shoot Uziyah despite his goading sneer and arched wings, we stared at each other in a hushed and awkward silence surrounded by the roar of circling jets and the *thwap-thwap-thwap* of helicopters.

"Remember how we adopted nearly two dozen angels after the apocalypse?" I shouted into the wind and rain and noise.

"Yeah…?" came the suspicious reply.

"Well, now we have all of them."

The rest of that night and the days following were a bit of a blur. We all crashed hard due to exhaustion. Except for Uziyah, because—warrior angel. We were kept under observation for a while. I had another panic attack. Or a breakdown. It was like my body decided we were done as soon as it knew we were safe. There was a lot of sedation and therapy. Only one of those is ongoing, at least.

Christmas was a sad affair without the angels. Without a certain angel. Lonely despite Steph and Greg and the Martello Court residents coming round to celebrate the anniversary of our victory. I didn't bother to untangle my ball of lights. I wasn't in a festive mood.

32

"Maia?"

Steph's voice drags me to the present. From the way she's looking at me—the way they're all looking at me—I suspect it's not the first time she's called my name.

I take a deep breath. My focus lifts to a monitor over the doctor's shoulder. Hunter's face fills the screen. An oxygen mask covers his mouth and nose, connected to a plastic gas canister of anaesthetic. Dark lashes brush his cheekbones, his black hair in a tangle over his forehead. Even blacker wings curl around the central cylinder of the MRI.

Steph gives my hand another squeeze. "We can pick someone else—"

I swallow the fear, and shake my head. "It wouldn't be right. Do it."

The doctor's nod sends her ponytail swishing. A throb vibrates from my feet to my bones like the thrum of the engines of the Protectorate ship. My grip tightens around Steph and Greg. Greg whines but Steph shushes him. I watch Hunter's face, my eyes wide and unblinking and starting to sting. My pulse rushes in my ears, my throat, my chest.

What if Uziyah was an anomaly? His cybernetics were already damaged. What if that's the difference between success and failure? Maybe we should have battered Hunter around the head before we put him in the machine.

It's my fault for trying to be fair with the random selection. Of course, Hunter drew the short straw to be the next test subject. Fuck you fate, or Sod's Law, or whatever. As soon as I saw his name, I had to bite my tongue to stop myself from demanding we use Abayankari instead.

An alarm bleeps. My stomach churns. The throb of the MRI fades.

"This is how it went with Uziyah, too," Steph says in the same placating tone. "Remember? We just wait for his tissues to cool then start again."

I nod, though my teeth are clenched. I force my hands to relax before I break my best friends' fingers.

The doctor explained it to us. MRI uses radiation in the radio frequency range, which can lead to heating when it's absorbed by tissues, especially around the cybernetics. They know how much heating is acceptable in a human patient so they've extrapolated that for the much sturdier constitution of a warrior angel.

It should be fine. Uziyah was fine.

Another beep. The thrum of the machine vibrates in the walls.

Uziyah awoke feeling calm and strange. He still calls me feeble creature because he thinks it's funny but he's definitely changed. I often find him pausing mid-sneer, confusion on his face, the ingrained behaviour no longer supported by the aggression from the cybernetics.

Will Hunter be the same? Will my Hunter be there when he opens his eyes or will it be the monster the Creators made?

And what if he never opens his eyes?

33

Hunter

A warrior wakes ready to fight yet my body is sluggish. Heavy. A similar sensation to regaining consciousness after stasis except I am on my back instead of vertical. But the space is too small to be the echoing and open emptiness of the sleeping quarters.

A cohort of Protectorate may be silent but I can always feel them. Sense their coiled aggression. Their intent. It prickles along my nerves.

Yet I am alone. No movement or presence stirs my awareness.

I keep my eyes closed, my breathing steady. There is a sharp scent. Chemical. Not the citrus odour of the stasis fluid or the rotting aftertaste of sedative gas. It is similar to when I was held in the research lab. Separated from Maia. My fierce and tiny human.

I did not like that.

Where is Maia?

I stay still when I want to leap to my feet and growl at the next lifeform I encounter. Demand to be taken to her. I must assess the danger. Plan my attack.

I flex my wrists and ankles, the movement unobtrusive enough to be missed if I am being observed. No constrictions or bindings pin my arms and legs. My wings droop between the hard surface against my back, the floor a metre or so away.

If I am not bound, am I in a cell? It will not hold me for long.

What do I remember last? The control room of our ship. The disappointment of Salam'ack'tai'moran and Tallai'sig'chai, overseers of our faction of the Protectorate. Maia's worried face. My hands on Uziyah—past tormentor when I had to hide what I wanted. The clamp of a collar.

My breathing remains steady. There is no weight at my throat, no press of composite into my skin. No pain. The throb of engines should be vibrating through my cells but there is nothing.

Where am I?

I open my eyes.

White ceiling, harsh fluorescent light. Something creaks near my feet. The air in the room swirls from a sudden pressure shift. Stuttered breaths frame the closing creak of the door. A hint of lavender sugar eases the tension in my gut. I sit up.

Maia. Wide eyes. Concern. Her pulse flutters in the delicate hollow of her collarbones.

My human. My *wife*.

I reach for her. She flinches.

She never flinches. Not from me. She stood her ground and fought me in the depths of Newhailes when I was at my most arrogant and dismissive. Pretending to be all I was not and slowly dying inside. She faced me with a sword, fearful yet defiant.

She was beautiful. The most fascinating creature I had ever seen. Then she poked me with her blade and changed my fate forever.

Fear alters her scent to something bitter and metallic. But why is she afraid? What has happ—

Memories assault me, each as sharp as the sword she slid between my ribs. It is like watching a movie of someone else's life. Someone who looks like me, sounds like me, moves like me.

But they do not act like me.

They are cold, cruel, aggressive. They hate what I love. They—

My insides twist. I have taken many punches to the abdomen in the span of years from my first awakening. This pain is worse.

I slide from the firm surface of the table. Maia jerks backwards a step, closer to the door as if she might flee. My knees strike the equally firm floor.

I used to only kneel in defeat. In servitude. She gave me a choice so now I only kneel for her.

Everything burns—my gullet, my eyes—but I do not have the anatomy to cry like a human. Instead, my shame and sadness flame beneath my skin.

"Maia," I whisper, my throat choked. "I hurt."

I bow my head.

I tried so hard. I am so much bigger, stronger. She is fragile and tiny. Perfect. It does not matter that I was not in control. I promised I would be gentle. She trusted me.

But I *hurt*.

34

The anguish in those words rips through my chest and gut.

I hurt.

The devastation on Hunter's face, before he bowed his head and hid beneath the fall of his black hair, banishes the lingering apprehension that screamed for me to run from him.

I never run from him.

"It's really you." My voice wobbles, already thick with tears.

He raises his gaze. Tortured, midnight-blue eyes meet mine. His dark wings are as hunched as the rest of him.

"Forgive me, Maia," he husks, "though I do not deserve it."

My feet move. I drop to my knees to mirror him, and bury my nose where shoulder meets throat. My blubbery inhale brings his crisp scent of ice.

"I missed you," I whisper.

His arms and wings come around me, the gesture and the feel of him, the warmth of him, tearing me open. I sob into his neck. Months of fear and trauma and grief pour out to dampen his laced shirt. His grip tightens just short of cutting off my air but he knows how to be gentle. He knows how much I can take.

I cry harder, not caring that everyone's watching behind one-way glass. There's a WACO guy outside the door holding a rifle loaded with iron. He promised he would wound, not execute, should Hunter wake in a human-killing mood.

My fingers knead the muscles of Hunter's back beneath the join of his wings. His hot, ragged breaths fan through my hair.

"I am so sorry, Maia," he says.

I shake my head, smearing my own snot and tears over my face since Hunter is dripping with them. I can't stop, either. I feel like I might sob until I pass out.

"It's not your fault," I manage to gasp. "None of it was your fault. You had no choice."

We hold each other until my knees throb against the un-yielding floor. Hunter is shaking in my arms. I'm shaking, but finally the tears dry to leave me elated and exhausted.

"Where are we?" he says, his lips brushing my temple.

"Earth. I stole the Protectorate ship."

The corner of his mouth twitches. "Of course you did."

"We found a way to destroy the cybernetics. They can never control you like that again."

Unless they get another collar on him.

I banish the thought with a shiver. Hunter snuggles closer.

"I want to go home," he growls.

He stands with me pressed to his chest. I can't help a squeak but I hook my legs around his hips to show my wholehearted consent. He strides for the door, only relaxing one arm from me to open it. The WACO guy skips away but has the sense not to aim his weapon. Steph and Greg peer around the doorway further down the corridor. Hunter spins on his heel to face them and I end up staring deeper into the facility. Hunter tenses.

"*Uziyah*," he snarls.

I twist to see, my cheek pressed to Hunter's.

Uziyah crowds the door behind Steph and Greg, and sneers at my warrior angel. *"Hunter."*

"You are civilised now?" Hunter cocks his head. "I still do not like you."

"I do not like you, either. But I like the human."

"She is *mine.*"

"I like her how humans like puppies—they are feeble and must be protected. They do not couple."

Hunter grunts. "I am taking her home."

"Human fucker," Uziyah says, his smile amused rather than mocking.

Steph, Greg and I are the only ones who hear the ghost of *moally tumsasha* under the words, courtesy of the translation fluid, which never seems to wear off.

Hunter prowls past the doorway and keeps going. I meet Steph's gaze over his shoulder.

"Phone me when Dev's awake."

She nods. "You sure you're okay?"

"I am now."

"Good to have you back, man," Greg calls as we turn out of sight.

Hunter walks through the maze of the facility without hesitation but then it's nothing compared to the labyrinthine corridors of the Protectorate ship. He once told me he could feel the sun and the moon so he's probably using that ability to guide himself out.

Military personnel and scientists scurry from his path. We reach the concrete steps leading upwards. Hunter bares his teeth at the cameras, and the two sets of steel-reinforced doors buzz open for him. The last one spills us into a bright and frosty January day. Mown grass and squat buildings stretch to the surrounding woodland in the Bush Estate south of Edinburgh.

The government facility was built following the apocalypse to better detain and study warrior angels, while also providing a secure location for a coordinated response to any new threat.

Hunter's wings snap out. His arms hold me secure against his body. He leaps towards the sky until the blue expanse fills my vision. He strikes out north-west with the uncanny confidence of a homing pigeon. I cuddle tighter against the chill and tell him everything that happened while he was unconscious. He stays silent. The muscles in his back flex beneath my hands. He makes no comment on the new addition to Arthur's Seat, now surrounded by a cordon that's always clustered with tourists.

Nerves nibble at my stomach.

Is he expecting intimacy when we get home? Or did he just want a private place to decompress and reconnect? I haven't thought much beyond the relief of having my Hunter back. I'm woozy from it. Or maybe it's the cold. Possibly the vertigo.

Am I ready for sex? I just want to hold him and never let go. Never lose him again.

He swoops lower. We tilt to vertical and he lands on our balcony at Martello Court, his bent knees absorbing the impact. The glass door slides open and shut. He props me on my feet in the living room and immediately steps away. My skin goosepimples at the sudden absence of his heat.

He stares at his feet, laced tight in his black, knee-high boots. His wings curl protectively to frame his broad shoulders and narrow hips, the long length of his legs.

Another kind of warmth fills me.

"Can I touch you?" he says softly, still looking at his feet.

My heart shudders at his uncertainty.

"Always," I say.

He peeks at me through his hair. "Do you… still want to touch me?"

My chest hitches.

"Always," I say.

35

Hunter doesn't move. I take a step towards him. His dark eyes watch me, his expression still uncertain yet full of longing. I pull the zirconium wedding band from my thumb. The planet and star sparkle in the light through the sliding door, the topaz gems glittering like unshed tears. Hunter holds out his hand and my semi-indestructible warrior angel husband is unable to hide the tremble.

"I love you, Hunter," I whisper.

I slide the ring onto his finger. He captures my hand.

"I love you, too, Maia," he says. "I am so sorr—"

My fingertips press on his lips. "No more apologies. It wasn't you. You would never hurt me."

My therapist has helped me work through a lot. We talked about my worries—blaming him, letting the bad memories wipe out all the good ones, never letting go of the fear.

I'm not afraid anymore.

I close the space between us and stretch up on tip-toe to replace my fingers with my mouth. A noise catches low in his throat. He kisses me back. A tentative glide of lips, not the usual frantic hunger of my warrior angel. His hands stay light on my shoulders.

"Touch me, Hunter," I say against his lips. "I want you to

touch me."

The noise becomes a groan. He grips my hips and hoists me upward without breaking the kiss. I wrap my legs around his waist. He licks my bottom lip, and I open for him. His tongue touches mine with an electric sizzle. The kiss becomes breathless and hot. I grind against the firm muscles of his stomach. He lowers me to the couch. All I can see is the flare of his wings until he leans back, settling on his haunches and looking up at me.

His fingers hesitate on the zip of my hoodie. "Can I?"

I nod, my mouth too dry to form the word.

It's like our first time—anxiety and lust warring together. Desperate to claim him yet terrified he'll hurt me by accident.

He eases my zipper down, never taking his eyes off me. Warm hands tug my hoodie and disappear my t-shirt, leaving me in my bra and jeans. Still Marks & Spencer but black and lacy. Hunter's fingertip traces the edge and tickles across the somewhat infinitesimal swell of my breasts. My heart thuds beneath his touch. He bends to kiss me, and my eyes flutter closed. His mouth trails along my jaw to nibble my ear. My head drops onto the couch back to give him better access, and he brands open-mouthed kisses down the column of my throat. I gasp when his tongue dips into the hollow between my collarbones, and again when he reaches my bellybutton. His mouth continues its exploration of my quivering stomach while his fingers unbutton my jeans and slide them off. He kisses my thighs, my knees, my feet. His hands wander while his lips map my body—ribs, hips, shoulders. He touches everywhere except the parts covered by thin lace and polyester.

It reminds me of the boiler cupboard—Hunter nothing but two scalding hands in the dark. The thrill, the anticipation, the utter eroticism of being manhandled by a horny, arrogant angel who knew exactly what he was doing when he slid his hand into my pants.

I bite my lip, struggling to keep myself still under Hunter's expert attention. He finally removes my underwear, and I'm naked on the couch while he's fully dressed and kneeling between my legs. Heat curls in my stomach. Muscles clench in glorious expectation.

I may hate them for knowing it but the other angels are right—Hunter is good on his knees. At least now he kneels because he wants to, not because he's forced to.

And he only kneels for me.

He nuzzles the curve of my boobs, his hands constantly stroking my sides, my arms, my waist but straying no further. He swirls his nose through my pubic hair. Scorching breath brushes the juncture of my thighs. I widen my legs but he ignores the invitation and traces a wet line down my leg with his tongue.

"*Hunter,*" I whine.

He sits on his heels and smirks at me. The sight of it is a fist to the throat. My eyes blur.

"Please, Hunter," I choke. "I need you. I missed you."

He cups my thighs and spreads me wider. "You have me, Maia. Forever and always."

His tongue laps between my legs, and I melt into the couch. No more teasing—he kisses me with the same fervour and attention he uses for my mouth. Sparks zing along my nerves and flare in my gut. I sob his name. He purrs against my sensitised flesh. The orgasm rips through me in a roar of tingles and heat. I arch over the sofa, my limbs flailing. It grinds me against Hunter's wicked mouth, prolonging the beautiful agony. He sucks and licks until I'm boneless and squirming.

I only realise my eyes are shut when I hear the rustle of his clothes. He takes a moment to caress the knife at my ankle. The same blade I had on the Protectorate ship.

I'm never going anywhere without at least one iron weapon ever again.

Hunter's tender hands switch our positions, scooping me into his lap. I blink at him, a knee on either side of his thighs. My very naked, very horny angel.

A wisp of fear tries to ruin the moment but I bat it away.

"You are in control so I do not hurt you," Hunter says, his hands lightly bracketing my hips. "I will never hurt you again."

"You never hurt me to begin with."

Wow, my voice is husky.

I steady myself on his shoulders. His wings flick against the couch, the length of them flattened against the cushions. His eyes are filled with warmth and affection, not cruelty and scorn. I slide down onto him. Slow and deep. There's no pain, only a familiar stretch and fullness. Our matching whimpers drift to the ceiling. His ends on my name. I roll my hips, and swallow the next. He meets me with careful thrusts despite his frantic, drugging kisses. I drive myself onto him. Harder, faster. I need his pleasure just as much as I need mine.

The Creators abused us both.

Hunter groans into my mouth, and I know he's close. Our rhythm falters, our bodies slick and quivering. We buck against each other. I yell his name and convulse in his arms. My forehead hits his shoulder, my body completely spent. He places a lazy kiss on my sweaty nape.

"Let's do that again," I murmur. "In about ten minutes."

He chuckles, and it vibrates to where he's still buried inside me. I writhe in his lap. He tilts his hips to stroke across aching flesh.

"I do not need ten minutes, Maia."

I groan. "Oh, fuck. Neither do I. Don't stop. Don't ever stop."

"Whatever you wish, my wife."

He circles his hips. Velvet wings brush fevered skin. I arch to meet him, another climax already barrelling my way.

And then my phone rings.

36

Hunter flies us to the underground facility in time to find Devinon sitting up on the metal table in the recovery room. Steph is lost beneath the blanket of his sapphire wings but her sobs echo in the narrow space. Greg hovers near the doorway, turning when Hunter and I enter. He glances at our joined hands and slides us a grin.

"So you two kissed and made up."

I wrinkle my nose. "We didn't have to make up."

"But I was right on the kissing part?"

"Shut up, Greg."

Man, it's good to have the whole gang back together.

Greg returns his gaze to the entangled Steph and Dev. A flash of longing crosses his face before he smothers it.

"Where is Uziyah?" Hunter says.

Greg seems happy at the distraction. "Pestering the good doctors to treat Abayankari next."

"He has a thing for her, doesn't he?"

Greg smiles at me. "Funny you should mention it. I asked him. He sneered and said he respects her as a warrior and is curious to see if she will be the same after the cybernetics are removed. He does, however, hope she will be less cruel."

"Considering what she wanted to do to me, I hope that, too."

"What did she want to do to you?" Hunter growls.

I pat his hand where we're linked together. "It doesn't matter anymore. After the MRI, she'll be a softer, calmer version of herself. Like Uziyah."

Hunter smirks. "I would like to be there when you tell Uziyah he is soft."

"Are you kidding? He's like six of me put together."

Hunter pulls me into his side and kisses my temple. I snuggle closer, taking the opportunity to sniff him.

"I am here now. He would not dare touch you. Though perhaps…" Remembrance darkens Hunter's eyes. "Perhaps I owe him an apology."

I squeeze his hand. "After what he did to you, I'd say you're both even."

Hunter tucks my back against his chest and rests his chin on the top of my head.

Steph sniffs loud and mucusy. She raises her face to reveal blotchy cheeks and red eyes.

"Greg, get over here, you idiot," she says. "Tell Dev how much you missed him."

"That's my cue," Greg says, blushing.

He scuttles across to Steph and Dev. The angel gives Steph a thorough snog before he lets her slip from the safety of his arms. Greg shuffles his feet.

"Uh… glad to have you back, man," he says, and punches Dev on the shoulder.

Steph rolls her eyes. Something passes between her and Devinon over Greg's awkwardly bobbing head. She nods, and nudges Greg closer to the angel. Dev cups Greg's face, stopping him mid-fidget.

"If you cannot say it I will—I missed you, prickly pear. And

I am sorry for the hurt I inflicted when I was not in control."

"That's, uh, that's okay. You can let go of my face now."

Dev's thumbs stroke Greg's cheeks. Greg squirms but doesn't pull away.

"You protected our delicate butterfly even from me," Dev says quietly. "I cannot thank you enough for that."

The angel lowers his head slowly, broadcasting his intent. Greg's eyes get wider, his face pinker, the closer Dev gets. Greg sucks in a breath. His eyebrows reach his hairline.

But he doesn't struggle.

Dev places a chaste kiss on the other man's lips. Barely a graze. Greg goes rigid then immediately limp. His whimper sounds as if he's been holding it in a long time. He buries his fingers in Dev's blond hair and puts his whole body into the kiss, grinding his hips into the other male. Dev's wings flare.

I tear my gaze away but can't block out the eager, wet moans. Steph watches her men, her hands clasped to her chest. Her eyes are shining, like she's just won free wigs for life.

"About goddamn time, you closeted idiot!"

She slaps Greg on the shoulder. Greg surfaces from the kiss, dazed and blinking, his brown hair ruffled from Devinon's fingers. Steph takes her beloved's lead and smooshes Greg's face between her palms, planting a kiss on his swollen lips. Greg's knees buckle. Dev scoops him into his lap, supporting him while Steph has a no-holds-barred exploration of his mouth until it seems Greg is ready to melt into a puddle.

"Time for us to go home," Steph says, coming up for air.

Greg splutters. "Oh god, oh fuck… yes, *fuck* yes."

"I think you broke Greg," I say.

Dev slides from the table still cradling the smaller man to his chest, and hustles for the door. Hunter executes a smooth side-step and spin to let them pass. Steph skips along behind, propelled by her cane. She pauses in the doorway but sends a longing glance towards her men striding down the corridor.

Well, one is striding. The other appears to have gone full cooked noodle.

"Did we have anything planned later?" she says. "I'm gonna be honest, Maia—I may not be available for the rest of the day. The week, even."

I match her smirk and yank her into a hug.

"Hey, big guy," she says to Hunter since she's now in his face. "She was a mess without you. Don't ever leave her again."

"Oh, come on, I wasn't—"

"They will regret taking me from her. I swear it on my life."

"That's what I like to hear."

I pinch Steph. She squeaks and scrambles backwards.

"If you're quite finished, I just wanted to say I'm happy for you. All three of you. You're meant to be together."

Steph manages to grin and blush at the same time. "I feel like the luckiest woman in all the universes."

"Then go. I'll talk to you later." I raise my voice as she limps off down the corridor. "And I want all the details!"

Hunter keeps cuddling me long after they've disappeared, the corridor empty. Footsteps squeak somewhere distant. A door clacks shut. I snuggle into Hunter's warmth, safe and content in his arms.

"It's not over, is it?" I say into the silence.

"No, Maia. It is not."

I sigh. "How did I end up the leader of another bloody rebellion?"

Hunter's lips curl against my hair. "You are good at it."

"Do you think we'll be ready for them?"

"Yes."

I wish I shared his confidence. We may not have broken this time but next time, they'll want more. They'll want blood—silver and crimson. And they'll hit us with everything they have.

Next time, they'll come to conquer.

Let Me Know What You Think!

Thank you for reading my book! I love hearing from my readers so please leave me a review.

Can't wait to hear from you!

For a bonus epilogue of Maia and Hunter out in the world turning mundane activities to badass adventures, join my mailing list at nadinelittle.com/bonus-epilogue by scanning the QR code below:

LITTLE PUBLISHING

Watch Out for the Next Book in the Series:
We Are Not Conquered

The final epic battle begins…

About the Author

Nadine Little lives in Scotland and is an ecologist who loves botany. This may be one of her few series without anything resembling a dragon. The story came about when she'd reached a snag in her novel *Verdana* and had no idea how it was going to end. As a break, she decided to write about the soothing topics of global catastrophe and surviving an angel apocalypse.

You're welcome.

For more on her books and a peek behind the scenes, sign up to her mailing list and follow her on social media.

You can connect with me on:
- https://nadinelittle.com
- https://twitter.com/Nadine_Little_
- https://www.facebook.com/nadinelittleauthor

Subscribe to my newsletter:
- https://nadinelittle.com/bonus-epilogue